Hank moved around the porch, aware that she was watching him.

The thought was exciting, and he felt a flush creep up his face as he realized that he found Stephanie a very desirable woman.

He knelt to examine the tear, just large enough to allow a big snake to slither through. "Where was the second snake?"

"In the sunroom." She hesitated. "The door was open. I just assumed that it must have been left that way."

Hank took a slow breath and examined the screen one more time. "I'm not trying to scare you, but I think someone cut the screen and let the snakes in. I think they left the door open, too."

"Why would someone do that?" she asked, her voice losing confidence.

He stood up and met her gaze. "To run you off."

Dear Harlequin Intrigue Reader,

Spring is in the air and we have a month of fabulous books for you to curl up with as the March winds howl outside:

- Familiar is back on the prowl, in Caroline Burnes's *Familiar Texas*. And *Rocky Mountain Maneuvers* marks the conclusion of Cassie Miles's COLORADO CRIME CONSULTANTS trilogy.

- Jessica Andersen brings us an exciting medical thriller, *Covert M.D.*

- Don't miss the next ECLIPSE title, Lisa Childs's *The Substitute Sister*.

- Definitely check out our April lineup. Debra Webb is starting THE ENFORCERS, an exciting new miniseries you won't want to miss. Also look for a special 3-in-1 story from Rebecca York, Ann Voss Peterson and Patricia Rosemoor called *Desert Sons*.

Each month, Harlequin Intrigue brings you a variety of heart-stopping romantic suspense and chilling mystery. Don't miss a single book!

Sincerely,

Denise O'Sullivan
Senior Editor
Harlequin Intrigue

FAMILIAR TEXAS
CAROLINE BURNES

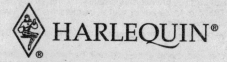

HARLEQUIN®

TORONTO • NEW YORK • LONDON
AMSTERDAM • PARIS • SYDNEY • HAMBURG
STOCKHOLM • ATHENS • TOKYO • MILAN • MADRID
PRAGUE • WARSAW • BUDAPEST • AUCKLAND

ISBN 0-373-22831-7

FAMILIAR TEXAS

ABOUT THE AUTHOR

Caroline Burnes has written seventeen books in her
FEAR FAMILIAR series. She has her own black cat,
Familiar's prototype, E. A. Poe, as well as Miss Vesta,
Gumbo, Maggie and Chester. All are strays and all
have brought love and joy into her life. An advocate
for animal rights, Caroline urges all her readers to
spay and neuter their pets. Unchecked reproduction
causes pain and suffering for hundreds of thousands
of innocent animals.

Books by Caroline Burnes

CAST OF CHARACTERS

Stephanie Chisholm—She has come home to Pecos, Texas, to settle her uncle Albert and aunt Emily McCammon's ranch estate. Once she returns to the small town she fled from years before, she realizes that her relatives may have been murdered and their cattle ranch stolen.

Hank Dalton—He is the rancher next door, a man who has learned the price of loving the wrong woman. He needs water on the McCammon ranch, and he's not too proud to ask for it. Once he meets Stephanie, his belief system is challenged.

Familiar—The cat returns to Texas to help a young woman unravel events that led up to her relatives' unexpected deaths.

Nate Peebles—A lawyer with a steadily growing list of "inherited" ranches.

Rodney Jenkins—He works on the McCammon ranch, and he's always in the wrong place at the wrong time.

Sam Hodges—Sheriff of Pecos, but with so much going on, should Stephanie trust him to help her, or is he bought and paid for by the people who are trying to kill her?

Johnny Benton—He was engaged to marry Stephanie, with her relatives' blessing. When she fled the ranch life and Texas for a high-powered career in advertising, did he truly understand? Or has he carried a grudge for years?

Jackie Benton—Johnny's wife of a decade. She seems eager to see Stephanie succeed in Pecos, but what truth lies beneath her smile?

Wanda Nell Hempstead—Works as a salesclerk, but she turns up all over town. What is her connection to the Bentons, and why does she hate Familiar so much?

Chapter One

The tumbleweed blowing against the cemetery fence is so-o-o appropriate. If Oliver Stone decided to do a movie set in Hell, he'd locate here in Pecos, Texas, a place that looks like the ends of the earth. Hot, dry, and desolate don't even begin to do it justice. The only thing worth looking at is Stephanie Chisholm, a woman with a lot of fortitude and grit, not to mention gams that could bring a guy to his knees. Look at her, standing with her shoulders squared and her jaw firm against the backdrop of funeral flowers and two open graves. Her dark curls are as wild and free as the Texas breeze. Even with grief in her eyes, she's a magnificent woman. I've only known Stephanie for two days, but I know her well enough to know this is breaking her heart, but not her will. She's come home to Texas to say goodbye to her uncle Albert and aunt Emily, the couple who raised her after her parents divorced—it seemed neither one wanted her. They were her real family, and now they're dead.

Dead in a very suspicious manner, I might add.

Stephanie faxed me the coroner's report—accidental death when a barn structure collapsed during a wind sheer. Right. I checked the Internet weather reports and Pecos, Texas, was the only town in the Southwest to suffer a wind sheer on May 26. Everywhere else in the region had perfect weather, except the one spot where the barn stood. Neighbors half a mile away didn't notice any bad weather. No, this killer wind blew out of a perfectly clear sky and collapsed a barn that had been standing for fifty years. Yeah, a freak, killer wind. Stephanie is right. There's something rotten in Texas.

Stephanie has come to the cemetery to pay her respects to her relatives, but I'm here to gather information. About fifty people are attending the gravesite rites. Some are obviously cowboys who worked for the McCammons. There's one who looks like a young Rowdy Yates, lean and muscular and filled with that peculiar cowboy grace. He's staring at Stephanie as if he'd never seen a woman, but she's too busy controlling her emotions to notice him.

Beside the cowboys are a little cluster of city folk who don't fit in at all. I look around and watch the mourners watching Stephanie. A few of the older attendees really seem upset at the deaths. There are some here, though, who arouse my suspicions. The way the McCammons died is one thing we're looking into. The other is this new will that suddenly turned up. Stephanie has been completely disinherited. There is no mention of the McCammons's plan to turn the ranch into a trust, something they'd often discussed with Stephanie.

Damn! Stephanie is crying. She isn't making a sound, but huge tears are running down her flawless cheeks. Behind her sunglasses, her hazel eyes are filled with pain. Let me give her a little kitty nuzzle and a love bite. There, that made her smile. She's pulling herself together, and just in time, too.

The minister is closing his service. So far, no one has spoken to Stephanie or offered a word of sympathy. The mourners are breaking up, and Stephanie is signaling me to join her at the Jeep we rented in Dallas. We're not going to escape unscathed, though; here comes a blond woman with a determined stride.

THE SUN BROILED the back of Hank Dalton's neck, and as soon as the prayer was over, he put his straw cowboy hat back on his dark curls, eager for the moment when he could remove the confining suit coat. Only his respect for Albert McCammon would have forced him into a black coat on a hot May day. Albert McCammon had been a genius with a herd of cows and some parched dirt. He'd spend many a hot day teaching Hank how to settle an injured cow or train a horse. And on those days, Albert had talked often of his niece, Stephanie Chisholm, a woman so beautiful the angels smiled in her presence and so smart she could accomplish anything she set her mind to.

Now, Hank found himself staring at the young woman, and she was even lovelier than Albert had described. He guessed her to be about thirty-five, a willowy five foot seven inches, with dark hair that looked like it was made for sensual moments spread across white sheets. For all of her beauty, she was struggling to hold back her tears. He liked the way she held herself straight, even though she had to know that everyone in town was talking about her, and the talk wasn't pleasant.

He shifted so that he could get a better view of her and noticed the black cat that seemed to lurk around her legs. What kind of woman traveled with a cat? He had a dog, Biscuit, a blue heeler that was indispensable working the cattle. But a cat? He wondered what Albert's heeler, Banjo, would think about a cat. What would become of Banjo? If Stephanie didn't want the dog, Hank would take him. In fact, Hank would be perfectly willing to take the entire McCammon Ranch. That was heavy on his mind as he stood among the mourners and listened to the service that concluded Albert and Emily's days on earth.

"I wouldn't be mooning after Stephanie Chisholm," Jackie Benton whispered in his ear.

Taken aback, Hank glanced at Jackie. The blonde was normally easygoing. Hank suddenly remembered the old gossip about how her husband, Johnny, had been dumped by Stephanie.

"What? Stephanie is a man eater?"

Jackie shook her head, her eyes dancing with amusement. "No, she's just a city girl. She doesn't have any use for the ranch life."

"Is that so?" Hank felt a glimmer of hope. Maybe Stephanie would sell the McCammon Ranch to him. If she wasn't interested in ranching, she'd have to do something with it. A ranch couldn't just look after itself.

"Her life is martini lunches, cocktail galas and art gallery openings. She'd die here."

"But she has a link to the land. This was where she grew up," Hank said, thinking about the thirty thousand acres that comprised the ranch. The big benefit to the McCammon land was Twisty Creek. Last year, Hank had an abundant water supply in the form of Charity Branch. But land developers had put in a subdivision north of his place and diverted the branch so that now, he was having to pump water in for irrigation and his cattle.

"From what Johnny told me, Stephanie *always* wanted to live in a city. Even as a teenager she was mooning and dreaming about the excitement of New York. She has her own advertising agency in New York now, along with her Fifth Avenue penthouse. She makes a ton of money—look at her. Those are designer clothes, and I should know. Look how they fit her. She's a dress designer's delight."

Hank couldn't tell if Jackie was envious of Stephanie or admiring. He cleared his throat and turned his attention to the minister, who was getting ready to say the last prayer before Albert and Emily were returned to the earth.

"I will say Stephanie has spunk," Jackie allowed. "Folks around town feel that she abandoned Albert and Emily. There was a betting pool going down at the café that she wouldn't even show up for the funeral. I guess she proved them wrong."

"I didn't live here when she was still in town, but I spent a lot of time with Albert. All I ever heard from him about her was a lot of praise. She made him proud."

"That's right," Jackie said. "I think I'll go over and invite her to the house for the meal."

STEPHANIE FOCUSED on the Jeep only twenty yards in front of her. If she could just make it, then she could close the door, drive away, and give in to the grief that threatened to overwhelm her. Uncle Albert and Aunt Emily were dead. She'd never see them again. She'd been away in New York when they needed her. The guilt and grief were so heavy Stephanie stumbled.

"Ms. Chisholm!"

She turned to face the blond woman barreling toward her. Stephanie took in her expensive black suit, the Italian heels and the hat with a veil which settled perfectly on short blond curls.

"Yes?" she said, knowing that she'd have to talk to people to find out what had really happened. But she'd never seen this woman before.

"Ms. Chisholm, I'm Jackie Benton, Johnny's wife."

Stephanie took an involuntary step back. She'd scanned the crowd and hadn't seen Johnny Benton, the man she'd been engaged to marry more than a dozen years before. The man she'd all but left at the altar when she'd run away to New York.

"Thank you for coming to the funeral," Stephanie said. "Did you know my aunt and uncle?"

"Oh, yes, very well. They were delightful people.

They came over to the house quite often on the weekends. They both adored Johnny. They looked at him like a son, and I think Emily was worn-out with cooking for the hands by the weekend. She enjoyed a break where I could pamper her a little."

Shame struck hard at Stephanie. This woman was a stranger, but she'd looked after Albert and Emily. "You were good to my aunt, thank you."

"Johnny felt like the McCammons were his second parents. And they were easy to be good to. They were some fine folks. Everyone in town is still in shock about their passing."

Stephanie started to say something about how they'd been murdered, but she felt the sharp claws of the cat digging into the top of her foot. Familiar was right. Now was the time for discretion, not bravado.

"Where is Johnny?" she asked.

"He's in Austin on a business trip. He just couldn't help it, otherwise he would have been here. Why don't you come out to the house? Some of the church people brought food there…" She hesitated. "They didn't know where else to bring the food. No one knew if you'd be home or not."

As much as it hurt, Stephanie realized Jackie was right. She hadn't kept in touch with a single person in town. Often not even her aunt and uncle. She'd been busy, focused on her career, forgetting that her relatives wouldn't always be around for her convenience.

"Thanks, but I want to go out to the ranch."

Jackie looked down at the ground. "That might not be a great idea."

"I have a lot of good memories there. I'll miss Uncle Albert and Aunt Em, but I'll be fine."

"It's just that…" She looked up and smiled. "Call us if you need us. We're only about five miles down the road."

"Thank you," Stephanie said as she got in the Jeep beside the panting cat.

STEPHANIE ALMOST RIPPED the door of the Jeep as she got out and stomped—as well as a girl could stomp in high heels—across the ditch to the For Sale sign that was prominently displayed at the gate of McCammon Ranch.

"Who in the world put this sign up?" she said aloud as she began to wrench the sign from the dry ground. "The will hasn't even been probated. Nothing can be sold until that's done."

When the sign wouldn't come up, Stephanie went back to the Jeep, got in and put it in Drive. In a moment there was the sound of splintering wood. She looked in the rearview mirror with satisfaction. The realty sign had been flattened. McCammon Ranch was not for sale. Not for any price, and certainly not until the will left by her aunt and uncle had been thoroughly examined. She glanced at the black cat in the passenger seat. He seemed to have a smirk of satisfaction on his face, too.

"The people responsible won't get away with this," she said aloud.

The cat turned a penetrating green gaze on her. "Meow." He nodded once to show he agreed.

"Thank goodness I heard about your P.I. agency, Familiar. Hiring you to help me unsnarl this whole mess was one of the smartest things I've ever done," she said as she turned the rental down the driveway. Her gaze was critical as she swept it over the graceful oaks that lined the driveway. The fences were good, the pastures as lush as they could be in a heat wave, but there were no cows. Not a single steer or heifer. No horses. Not even a dog. A creepy sensation slipped over Stephanie. Where was all the livestock? She'd talked to her uncle only a week before, and he'd told her the spring calves had arrived without a single loss. So where were they?

She drove slowly down the winding driveway. The old white farmhouse came into view, and Stephanie again fought back tears. She'd managed to hold herself together at the funeral service because she had no intention of giving the lot of Nosey Parkers the satisfaction of seeing her cry. Now, though, there was no one to see her but the black cat, and Familiar seemed to have a real streak of compassion.

As soon as she stopped the Jeep, the cat was clawing at the window to get out. She opened her door and he shot out by her feet. "Hey," she called. "Don't get lost." But it was too late—the tip of his tail disappeared in the shrubbery by the front porch.

For a moment Stephanie indulged her memories. The last time she'd come home, nearly a year ago, Aunt Emily had met her at the door, the wonderful scent of baking apple pies wafting out on the breeze. Uncle Albert had come in from the barn, wiping his hands on an old towel so he could give her a hug without smudging her designer suit. She closed her eyes and relished the memory, determined to hold her aunt and uncle close to her in her heart if not in her arms.

"Ms. Chisholm?"

She whirled at the unexpected voice behind her.

"Who are you?"

"I'm Rodney Jenkins. I was your uncle's chief wrangler. I just wanted to tell you how sorry I am for your loss. I didn't want to go to the funeral." A frown crossed his face. "I was afraid I'd have to deck some of those folks."

"Rodney, where are the cows?"

His frown deepened. "You don't know?"

She shook her head, aware that she dreaded his answer.

"They were sold at auction yesterday. The whole herd. The man who bought them came and got them this morning."

Stephanie felt as if she'd been gut-shot. "Every cow?"

"And the horses. They were sold as a lot. Even your uncle's blue heeler. They took old Banjo."

The sensation of disbelief was quickly replaced by sheer, unadulterated fury. "Who did this?"

"It wasn't the fault of the men who came for the cows," Rodney said, kicking the dirt with his cowboy boot. "It was Nate Peebles, a local lawyer, who ordered the cows sold. He's the one put up the For Sale sign you flattened coming in." He smiled. "Good work."

"McCammon Ranch isn't for sale. Not now. Not ever." She was surprised at the passion of her words. Not so long ago she'd fled the ranch, terrified that she'd spend her days cooking three meals a day for hungry ranch hands and her nights birthing calves and tending to sick stock.

Rodney held out his hand. "I'll shake on that, Ms. Chisholm. Now tell me what I can do to help."

Stephanie was about to answer when she heard a long growl and a feline howl of outrage. "What in the world?" She started toward the house with Rodney at her heels.

The cry came again, this time louder. Stephanie began to run. She rounded the corner just in time to see the rattlesnake lunge at the black cat. Familiar did an amazing leap into the air that ended in a flip on top of a rocking chair on the porch. Stephanie focused on the snake. It was at least six feet long. It moved toward the chair, its focus on the cat.

"Damn, it's a timber rattler," Rodney said as he drew his pistol out of his holster. "How'd it get inside the screen on the porch?"

"That's a very good question," Stephanie said cautiously. The snake had coiled. The tip of its tail, with fourteen rattles, quivered in the air giving the famous warning that the snake was about to strike.

"Don't move, Familiar." Stephanie opened the door and moved slowly onto the porch. "I'm going to distract it, Rodney, and then you shoot it."

"I might chip up the porch some."

Stephanie shook her head. "Blow the porch up, I don't care, just kill the snake."

As soon as she moved toward the snake, Rodney shot. He caught the snake in the head, and Stephanie scooped Familiar into her arms. She headed to the front door, and to her surprise, it was already open. She pushed the door gently, aware that Familiar was tensing in her arms.

"Yarrr-rrr." His fur was standing on end and he hissed into the open doorway, alerting her to the fact another snake—possibly more—was inside.

"Rodney, I think you'd better bring your gun," she said, feeling the knot of fear that had lodged in her gut. Rattlesnakes were always a danger, but none were more dangerous than those trapped inside a house.

"Ms. Stephanie, you come on out of there. I sure wish Banjo was here. He'd know what to do. That dog would ride out with your uncle, and if he came across a snake, he'd snatch it right behind the head and shake it until he broke its neck."

"I'll be getting Banjo back. And the cows. And the horses." The spur of anger helped her overcome her fear. She walked to the screen and put Familiar out on the grass. "No matter how much you want to help, you'd only be one swallow for a big rattler. Now stay outside. Rodney and I will kill it. You did your job by giving the warning."

Rodney lifted his hat and scratched his forehead. "Ms. Stephanie, do you always talk to your cat like that?"

She laughed. "Familiar isn't my cat. He belongs only to himself, but I do talk to him."

"Well, I can't speak to his intelligence, but he sure did good to warn us about the snakes."

Stephanie didn't push the issue. If Rodney agreed to

work with her, he'd have plenty of opportunity to see how smart the highly-rated feline detective could be.

"How do you want to handle this?" she asked Rodney.

He reached into his boot and brought out another gun. "I assume you know how to use this?"

Stephanie felt the heft of the pistol in her hand. Her uncle had spent a lot of time teaching her to shoot—and not to shoot. He'd explained that timing was everything in using a weapon. She sighted down her arm. "I used to be a pretty good shot. I'm a little out of practice."

"Just don't tell the snake," Rodney said, grinning. "Now let's get 'im."

They eased into the house, walking softly and listening. They'd made it only as far as the sunroom when she heard the warning rattle. The snake was under a chaise. Rodney signaled that he'd move the piece of furniture so she could shoot the snake.

Stephanie got down on one knee, sighting on the coils of the snake. She had to hit it clean, and in the head, preferably. She was in little danger, halfway across the room. Rodney was the one she had to protect.

"Ready?" he asked as he moved closer to the wicker chaise.

"Go."

He grasped the chaise and lifted it high. As he stepped back, the snake lunged. Stephanie pulled the trigger. The snake fell, writhing on the floor, headless.

"Nice shooting," Rodney said, putting the chaise across the room. "I'll get a shovel and take care of this mess. It's a good thing your aunt Em wasn't around.

She'd have both our hides for shooting into the wall like that." He pointed to the bullet hole.

"Aunt Em would have shot the snake herself." Stephanie smiled, but the pain of her loss was suddenly too much to bear. She felt the tears welling.

"Emily spoke of you all the time," Rodney said, his own eyes growing moist. "She was as proud of you as a new cow with a calf. She had a bulletin board in the barn, and she'd cut clippings from the *New York Times* when you had advertising successes."

Stephanie managed to gain control of her emotions. "Thank you, Rodney. But I should have been here, helping them."

He shook his head. "No, ma'am, now I have to disagree. Your aunt said you were doing what you needed to do at the time. 'Course she always felt you'd come home to Pecos and run the ranch when you got the city out of your blood."

"I just never thought I'd have to do it without them."

Chapter Two

Hank Dalton idled his truck at the gates of McCammon Ranch and studied the wreckage of the realty sign listing the property for sale. He understood a little more about the woman who'd occupied his thoughts for the last three hours. She might be a city woman with no interest in ranching, but she wasn't going to be pushed by anyone. Stephanie Chisholm wasn't going to give up McCammon Ranch until she was good and ready to do so.

He'd come to make her an offer on the ranch. He was going to be honest with her and tell her about the water situation on the Running Z. If she didn't want to sell, he was going to see if he could work out some grazing rights on land that bordered Twisty Creek. The water situation was serious for him. As much as he would have liked to give her time to grieve her loss, he didn't have time. He'd filed a lawsuit against the developers who'd rerouted the creek, but the legal system was too slow. His cows would be dead and his pasture land a desert by the time the courts ruled. He gazed at the tree-lined driveway and remembered the many happy times he'd driven over for dinner with Albert and Em.

He started down the driveway when he heard a gunshot. Pressing the accelerator to the floor, he pushed the truck to the maximum as he sped toward the white ranch house. As he pulled into the yard he saw Rodney coming out of the house with a huge timber rattler hanging off a shovel.

"Ms. Stephanie clean blew his head off," Rodney said proudly.

"How the hell did that snake get into the house?" Hank asked. "Albert never said he had a problem with rattlers."

"Good question. There was another one on the screened porch," Rodney said. "This one was in the sunroom. I don't recall Albert ever saying anything about snakes getting into the house, now that you mention it. Maybe the drought drove 'em inside looking for water."

Hank walked to the porch, wondering who had a key to the ranch house. "They had to get in some way, and wherever they came from, we need to find it and block it off."

"Let me bury these varmints and I'll be back," Rodney said.

Hank knelt down by the porch and began to run his fingers along the screen where it met the wooden floor. He was halfway round when he sensed someone watching him. He looked up into stormy hazel eyes.

"Who are you?" Stephanie asked.

Hank stood, taking in everything about her. She'd changed into jeans and a sleeveless gingham top that showed off slender arms with well-developed muscles. She might be a city girl, but she looked like she could hold her own with farm activities. He smiled. "I'm your neighbor to the north, Hank Dalton."

"Mr. Dalton." She held out her hand. "Uncle Albert and Aunt Em spoke of you. Thank you for attending the funeral."

"Albert and Em were very good to me." He sighed. "I hate to bring this up today, just after you buried your relatives, but I'm in something of a predicament."

"Would you like to come in?" she asked.

"Let me finish checking this screen." He bent back to his work. "Those snakes had to have gotten in somehow." He moved around the porch, aware that she was watching him. The thought was exciting, and he felt a flush creep up his face as he realized that he found Stephanie a very desirable woman.

"Those snakes scared the life out of me," she said, walking along the inside of the screen as he checked outside.

"I'll bet. Timber rattlers aren't known for their pleasant dispositions. How'd you find them?"

"The cat. Familiar. He warned us before we came in."

He couldn't help it. He stopped and stared at her. "That black cat that was with you at the funeral?"

"That's the one."

"Where's Banjo?" Hank bent to the task.

"He was sold. Along with the cows and horses."

As she spoke, Hank found the tear in the screen. He stood up slowly. "Banjo was what?"

"Sold."

They stared at each other, and he read her cold anger. "By whose directive?"

"I intend to find that out," she said. "And then I'll get back the cows and the horses. And Banjo. I can't believe they sold my uncle's cow dog."

"I was going to offer to take him if you didn't plan on staying at the ranch. He's friends with my dog, Biscuit, and I'd give him a good home."

"I have to get him back first."

He could see she was being very closemouthed about her plans, and he didn't blame her. Who in the hell would sell the stock on the ranch and even the dog? "Do you have any extra screen? I can patch this tear for you. Come sundown, you'll want it tight. The mosquitoes here are big enough to carry you off."

"I remember that," she said. "I'll get Rodney to patch it."

"No problem. I'll be glad to do it. A neighborly service." He knelt and began to examine the tear. It was a perfect square, just large enough to allow a big snake to slither through. "Where was the second snake?" he asked.

"In the sunroom?"

"How did it get into the house?"

She hesitated. "The door was open. I just assumed that Uncle Albert must have left it that way."

Hank took a slow breath and examined the screen one more time. "Ms. Stephanie, I'm not trying to scare you, but I think someone cut the screen and let the snakes in. I think they left the door open, too."

"Why would someone do that?" she asked, her voice losing some of its confidence.

He stood up and met her gaze. "To run you off."

SHE FOUGHT back emotion as she got the coffee pot, filled it with water and made coffee for Hank and Rodney. How many thousands of times had she watched her aunt Em do the whole process, smiling over her shoulder as she did so. She missed her aunt so terribly that she thought she'd double over with pain. Whenever she got control of herself, she was confronted with the harsh question: Why had she run away from this life? Why had she left the only two people who'd truly loved her throughout her entire life?

She felt a gentle hand on her shoulder, and before she knew what was happening, Hank had turned her into his chest. His strong arms circled her, holding her gently.

"Crying's about the only cure for grief," he said softly. "You pen it up inside you and it's going to cause a lot of damage later on."

She was too far gone to stop herself anyway. She'd held it all in, until now. She'd endured the long flight home, the funeral, the emptiness of the house, but now, she couldn't hold back any longer.

Hank's hands rubbed gently up her back as she sobbed against him. She was bitterly angry and guilty and sad. The emotions ruled her, and she cried, soaking the front of Hank's shirt. When the tears finally stopped, she stepped back and shook her head. "I'm so sorry. I don't even know you."

"We both loved them. I can't tell you the times Em made coffee for me, just like you were doing. If you hadn't started crying, I probably would have."

His words were unreasonably comforting. Stephanie finished setting up the coffee and turned on the pot. She took a seat at the table, her aunt's place, and saw the recognition in Hank's eyes.

"I know you came here for a reason, but can I ask one question first?"

"Sure."

He'd made his face expressionless. She wondered what he thought she was going to ask. "Were Uncle Albert and Aunt Em happy?"

The smile that spread across his face was instantaneous. "They were lucky people, in many ways. They loved each other and they were a team on this ranch. Albert worked and Em worked right beside him. I was lucky to see those two together. I always thought that kind of partnership was a lot of romantic sh—hooey. But it was real with them. Albert would go out to check the cows and long about noon, I'd see this horse coming in the distance and it would be Em. She'd have a picnic lunch packed for everyone. How she knew where to find us, I can't say."

"You worked with Uncle Albert?"

"We worked together. He had good hands, but a ranch can't run under a hired hand. He knew that. I had the same problem, so after the hands were through for the day, we often ended up finishing together."

"Did they…" She faltered. "Did they miss me too much?"

His face softened. "They talked about you all the time. About how you could live in any world you chose. They wanted you to come home, but only if that was your choice."

"I should have come home," she said, feeling the pressure of another bout of tears.

"Not unless the ranch was the life you want to live." He reached across the table and touched her hand. "Stephanie, this is a hard life. The stock and the ranch always come first. If you aren't willing to make that choice, you don't need to try to live it. Your folks knew that."

They both heard the screened door slam and they sat back. Rodney walked into the house. "The snakes are buried, but I have to say that ground is baked harder than a brick."

Stephanie rose to get him coffee. "Mr. Dalton found the hole in the screen." It felt odd calling him something other than Hank, especially with a huge dark stain on his blue shirt where her tears had soaked him.

"Rodney, I think someone cut the screen and put the snakes in the house."

"Who would do such a thing?" Rodney eased into a chair, worry on his face.

"Good question. Who's been around here lately?"

"The real estate man was here. He had a key to the house. Johnny Benton came around yesterday, with his wife. They said they'd come to tidy the house in case folks came out here. Someone had to get the clothes for Albert and Em." He looked stricken at the pain that crossed Stephanie's face. "Sorry, Ms. Stephanie."

She put a hand on his shoulder. "Not your fault, Rodney. It's my fault that strangers had to pick out my folks' funeral clothes."

Disapproval crossed Hank's face, followed by sorrow. He started to say something, then closed his mouth.

"I'll give you a hand patching the hole. Then we'd better check the rest of the house."

"If there was another snake, Familiar would have warned us."

Hank let a chuckle escape. "A snake cat. Now I've seen it all."

"Familiar is a lot more than that," Stephanie said, and she finally felt the darkness shift from her heart. "He's a detective."

"Like a private eye?" Rodney was laughing.

"Exactly. And I've hired him to look into the murder of my aunt and uncle."

Rodney paled. "Murder? It was an accident. That building collapsed on them."

A heavy silence settled on the table. Rodney sipped his coffee. "It was sort of strange," he said at last. "Not a cloud in the sky."

"What time did it happen?"

"About 1:30 in the afternoon." Rodney frowned. "Em normally wasn't outside at that time, but she musta gone to help Albert with that old tractor. It was giving him fits. We'd all gone up to the Twisty Creek pasture to ride the north fences. There'd been a lot of trouble with someone cutting the wire."

Stephanie kept her face carefully blank. "How long had that been going on?"

"About four weeks," Hank answered. "They were cutting the fence between the Running Z and McCammon. Just about every other day we'd have to separate the herds. It was becoming very annoying."

"Did you ever catch who was doing it?"

"We never could get 'em. We found some tire tracks and the sheriff sent out a deputy to make a mold, but we never heard a thing about it. 'Course Albert and Em were killed…" His sentence trailed off.

He didn't have to finish. No one was interested in catching fence vandals after the tragedy of a double death. Stephanie felt Hank's gaze on her, and she stared at him. His eyes were as green as a winter rye pasture, set perfectly in his rugged face. His dark hair contrasted with his tanned skin, completed with a straight nose and lips that made her think of the pleasures of kissing.

"I'll check with the sheriff and see what he matched with those molds," she said, clearing the thoughts of Hank from her mind.

"Rodney, we still have a few hours of light. Why don't we ride those fences?" Hank asked.

"Sure thing. To be honest, I'd be glad of the company. Not much cause to check the fences now, though. The cows are gone."

Hank's smile was lopsided. "That's right. The only

harm would be that my cows could get some water from Twisty Creek."

Stephanie realized then what he'd come to ask her. "Hank, you're welcome to the creek and the pasture until I get Uncle Al—*my* cows back." She saw his eyebrows lift at her emphasis. "But you might still want to ride that fence. We need to collect evidence, and the wind coming up this evening might destroy it."

"Let's search the house and get busy," Hank said. He put his coffee cup in the sink and headed through the dining room with Rodney.

The door closed behind them and Stephanie began to clean up the kitchen. Through the closed door, she heard Rodney's voice.

"She's smart *and* she's pretty, Hank. Wonder why she ain't married?"

THE HOUSE HAD BEEN FREE of additional snakes. Only the black cat had been found, asleep, in the bedroom that had to be Stephanie's. The room had been done in pale ivory eyelet lace, the carpet a dark beige. It reflected a certain sophistication, even for the nineteen-year-old girl who'd lived in it. The pale blond furniture would not be the taste of most young girls, and Hank realized it even as he lifted the dust ruffle and checked under the bed. An old pair of cowboy boots caught his eye and he pulled them out. They were well-worn, the heels rounded and the toes scuffed. He put them back and turned to the closet.

Several formal gowns reflected high school dates

and glory. He moved a few abandoned pairs of shoes and determined the closet was empty of snakes.

"Meow."

He turned to find the black cat watching him. He didn't believe a word that Stephanie had said about the cat's detective agency, but he found the feline's stare unsettling. It was as if the cat were assessing him. Maybe that was just a cat's personality. He was a dog man—no use for sleeping critters too lazy to even catch a mouse.

He stepped past the cat and felt a sharp, intense pain in his calf. He looked down and saw the cat had deliberately snagged him. "Hey!"

Familiar turned him loose and trotted back to the closet. "Meow."

He had the strangest sense the cat wanted to tell him something. "What's wrong?" he asked. "Timmy in the well?"

The cat gave him a long hiss.

"So, for all your many talents, you don't appreciate Lassie jokes?" He realized too late that he was talking to the cat as if it could understand him.

"Meow." Familiar disappeared in the open closet and began to scratch at the carpet.

"I think that's a reason to get evicted from the house," Hank said, walking over to catch the cat. He'd put him outside and let him scratch some tree trunks or fence posts.

He leaned into the closet and saw that Familiar had moved several pairs of shoes. He clawed at the carpet. Curious, Hank got down on his knees. The carpet had been pulled loose from the corner of the closet, and not by the cat. He lifted the flap, pulling it out to reveal a trap door. Hank hesitated only a moment before he pulled the door free and looked down to see the ground below the house. It was an escape hatch. In case of fires, he supposed.

He looked at the cat. It did seem the feline had known about this and decided to show him. "I'll get a board and nail it up," he said. If someone was sneaking around McCammon Ranch, he didn't want them to be able to slip into the house. The cat's gaze was so intense, he found he couldn't look away. At last he realized what the cat wanted. "Okay, thank you," he said, flipping the carpet back and feeling like the biggest kind of fool for talking to a cat.

He found an empty-handed Rodney at the other end of the house. They walked out together, headed for the barn.

THE OLD OAK BOX was still tucked in the wall safe behind the Remington where Uncle Albert had always left it. Stephanie carefully removed it from the safe and carried it to the kitchen.

Her heart lurched painfully, but she kept the tears at bay. Everything about the ranch held a memory. Most of them the best in her life. She'd cried enough, though, her face against Hank's strong chest. In all of her years in New York, she'd never felt as safe as she had those few moments in Hank's arms. That, she thought with a crooked grin, was the illusion of the cowboy. It was true they were men of honor who could be counted on for a dramatic rescue. She'd never known braver men than those who worked with her uncle on the farm. She'd seen them risk life and limb for a few moments of glory on a thrashing bull or rodeo bronc. The local weekly rodeo would start at eight Friday night in Pecos. She had half a mind to ride out there and watch for a little while. Maybe, along the way, she'd ask around to see who'd bought her uncle's cows.

She put her mind back on the task of getting the will. She'd known about the document since she was fifteen years old, when Albert had sat her down and explained what a will was and where he was putting it. He was a man who took care of loose ends.

She took a breath, willing herself to be calm, and opened the box. A sheaf of letters and documents covered the top. Beneath that was Aunt Em's jewelry. Stephanie blinked the tears away and lifted the papers out. She couldn't look at the jewelry. Not now. She didn't want to see the emerald pin that Albert gave Em on her fortieth birthday. It was in the shape of a clover, for good luck.

Trying to shut out the memories, Stephanie sorted through the documents. She was surprised to find letters from Albert to Emily. The date was 1961, and the postmark was from Pecos, Texas, to the University of Texas in Austin, where Em had gone to college. There were at least sixty letters, all bundled with a ribbon. Stephanie put them aside to read later, when her heart wasn't so wounded. At last she found the will. She hadn't realized how much she'd been afraid the document was gone until her fingers curled around it. She opened it up and read the simple terms. The ranch and all contents had been left to her with the instruction that she create a trust.

She gazed out the window and saw Hank and Rodney riding off on two of Rodney's personal horses. Thank goodness for the wrangler. There wouldn't be a grazing animal on the place if he hadn't kept his own.

The empty fields made her think of the terms of the trust. Albert had seen the handwriting on the wall. Subdivisions and developments had begun to eat away at the ranches. Land was more valuable for a home site than a pasture, so he'd left instruction in his will that Mc-Cammon Ranch remain a working ranch. The profits from cattle sales were to be plowed back into the ranch, for hands and materials to keep it going. The house, should Stephanie choose not to live in it, would be the residence of the ranch foreman.

It was a gift to future generations of Texans, those who might never see a working ranch, except for one created by a trust.

Stephanie gripped the document tightly. She had every intention of seeing Albert's dream come true. Now all she had to do was find out what in the hell was going on and who in the hell had put a For Sale sign on the ranch.

She went to the phone and dialed information for Kemper Realty, the firm on the sign. In a moment she was talking to the realty receptionist.

"Who listed McCammon Ranch?" she asked.

"That would be Todd Hughes," the woman said. "Would you like to speak to him?"

"More than you'll ever know," she said sweetly.

In a moment she heard a baritone voice identifying himself as Todd Hughes.

"I'm Stephanie Chisholm," she said, listening to the silence on the other end. "I just ran over a For Sale sign on my ranch. What can you tell me about it?"

"Ms. Chisholm?" There was disbelief in his voice. "I had no idea you were in town. I was led to believe you wouldn't be coming for the funeral. Where are you staying?"

"In my home."

There was another long pause. "I believe you need to talk to Nate Peebles."

"Who the hell is that?" she asked, her voice still sugary sweet.

"He's an attorney." Hughes cleared his throat. "He owns McCammon Ranch. Or at least he will when the will is probated. He's the one who told me to put up the sign."

Stephanie dropped into one of Uncle Albert's handmade chairs. "He what?"

"Albert McCammon left the ranch to him. I saw the will myself. The process of probating it has already been started. It's just a matter of time before—"

"He ordered the livestock sold?" Stephanie knew she was shouting and didn't care. In the bottom of her heart, she'd thought it was a mistake. That someone, acting on Albert's best interests, had taken it upon themselves to sell the stock. She'd thought it would be a matter of explanation and everything would be put right. Now, she saw her assumption had been wrong. Dead wrong.

"Mr. Hughes. I have my uncle's will in my hand. It states clearly the ranch goes to me, so that I can establish a working ranch trust, per my uncle's wishes. I advise you to take the ranch off the market. Now tell me who has the livestock?"

"I didn't handle that sell."

"Who has the cows? And the horses. And Banjo."

"Avis McElhanney."

"And where would I find him?"

"He has a place down on County Road 17."

Stephanie had a bad feeling. "A ranch."

"Not exactly. It's a holding lot for the meat packers."

Stephanie didn't bother with a goodbye. She slammed the phone down, returned the will to the wall safe and ran out of the house. Behind her, Familiar came at a dead gallop. By the time she opened the truck door, the cat flew past her and into the passenger seat.

Stephanie tore down the driveway, the SUV slewing in the gravel as she made a curve. She had to get to McElhanney's before the cows were either killed or loaded into transport trucks. Those red Angus cows were Albert's pride and joy. If anything bad happened to those cows, she was personally going to dig out Nate Peebles's heart with a spoon.

Chapter Three

Hank had ridden the western fence line while Rodney rode east. The wind had begun to pick up a little, and Hank was glad for the breeze. It was still hot, but at least the air was moving. He'd chosen Flicker, a red roan mare, from the six horses Rodney kept in the McCammon barn. She was a willing mount with an easy trot and tireless energy.

The land dipped slightly and he came off the rise and reined Flicker to a stop. He couldn't believe it. The fence was still up, but obviously not for long. A bulldozer sat against the fence, perched to plow it down.

"What the hell is going on?" he asked himself as he rode up to the piece of heavy equipment. No one was around. It was as if the dozer had been driven to the ends of civilization and then abandoned. But he knew better. Someone would be back, and in a matter of minutes, that person could rip out what would take months to replace. He slipped the key to the dozer into his pocket and followed a heavy set of tire tracks that led out. Someone had brought the dozer, unloaded it and left.

Hank had no doubt the intended target for the dozer was the fence. There wasn't anything else around to take down. He turned Flicker to the east and headed back to the ranch at a gallop. Someone was dismantling McCammon Ranch as fast as they could. Like it or not, Stephanie was in for a real fight.

When he pulled up to the barn, Flicker was tired and hot. After dismounting, he uncinched the mare's girth and walked her to cool her.

"Hank, thank goodness you're back!"

He turned to see Stephanie running across the barnyard toward him. He lifted the saddle off Flicker's back with one hand and carried it into the tack room. "What's wrong?" he asked, turning to face her.

"Uncle Albert's cattle are at McElhanney's feed lot. They're going to be killed in the morning."

Hank's mouth was a tight line. "I don't think so. Those cows were sold illegally, from what you tell me. Hop in my truck. We'll ride over to McElhanney's and see what they have to say."

When Stephanie opened the truck door, the black cat leapt inside. Hank gave the cat a look. "Biscuit's going to be very irritated when he smells cat in his truck."

"Familiar has to go." Stephanie sighed. "Sorry. That sounded very bossy. The cat needs to hear all of this."

Hank got into the truck and started the engine. "Avis McElhanney has run his feed lot and slaughterhouse for the past twenty years. I wouldn't sell a dead coyote to him, but he's convenient. The way he treats animals is a shame. Did you find out who sold the cows?"

"I did." She looked out the window, and he knew she was composing herself. He could only imagine what it would be like to come home for funerals and then find the place she expected to inherit being sold out from under her. "A man called Nate Peebles. Do you know him?"

"Some folks call him a lawyer. I think that's too classy a label."

Hank turned onto County Road 17 and he pressed the gas pedal to the floor. "Hang on. Tell me about the will Peebles claims to have."

Stephanie's jaw squared. "He says Uncle Albert and Aunt Em left everything to him. Every single thing."

Hank was stunned by the idea of it. "That's impossible. Albert meant to leave it all to you. He said so more than once. He said maybe you'd come home and run the ranch like you'd been taught."

Stephanie felt the wind whipping through the window and was glad that it dried her tears before she could shed them. "Peebles says the will I have isn't legal. There was a new will. One Uncle Albert signed just before he died. Peebles says there's nothing I can do."

"What about the cows?"

Her jaw had firmed and her eyes were hard and dry. "I have enough money to buy them." She turned to him. "Could I put them at your place until I decide what I'm going to do? We could mix the herds and let them all stay by the creek."

It was the most sensible solution. The same solution that Albert would have made, had he been alive. He cast a glance at Stephanie. With her perfectly shaded makeup, her expensive earrings and her manicured fingernails, she didn't look like a rancher. But she thought like one. She had that same generous spirit and determination that had allowed cattle ranchers to stay in business for decades. He was developing a healthy respect for her, and Hank Dalton didn't give his respect out lightly.

In the distance he could see the ramshackle barn where McElhanney kept his livestock standing in manure and filth until he was ready to either kill them or load them onto trucks to ship. Hank pulled beneath the shade of a dying pecan tree.

"Stephanie, this isn't going to be pretty. Maybe you should stay here. I'll be glad to negotiate to get your cows back."

"Where are they?" She got out of the truck and slammed the door. "If he's harmed them in any way…"

Hank accepted he wasn't going to be able to protect Stephanie. She'd grown up on a ranch. She knew what was what. He motioned for her to follow him as he led the way to the office. Maybe they could set a price and he'd arrange to have the cattle shipped in the morning.

Stephanie strode into the office with Hank and the black cat one step behind her. Hank had to hide a smile as he watched her walk to the desk, put her hands on her hips and lean down into Avis McElhanney's surprised face.

"You have my uncle's herd of red Angus. I want them back. Now."

McElhanney's surprise turned to bluster. "I bought

those cows fair and square. They're mine. They're due to be shipped out tomorrow."

"How much did you pay for them? I'll buy them back."

Hank lounged against the door frame. It didn't look like Stephanie needed any help. She was doing just fine.

"Twenty thousand dollars." McElhanney's grin was smug. "Take it or leave it."

Hank straightened up, ready to do whatever was necessary.

"That's outrageous," Stephanie said.

McElhanney smiled. "You want the cows back, that's what you're going to pay for them."

"Ten sounds more reasonable." Stephanie reached into her back pocket and brought out a checkbook. "I'll give you a check for ten right this minute."

"Twenty, or I'll call in my staff and butcher the whole lot tonight." McElhanney's smile widened. "Seems to me like I have the upper hand in this negotiation, little lady."

Hank stepped past Stephanie, leaned across the desk and grabbed McElhanney by the shirt collar. He snatched him out of his chair so hard the man was across the desk and standing on his tiptoes in front of Hank. "I want to see the bill of sale you have for the cattle. Now."

"Well, I don't—I didn't get a bill."

"Stephanie, pick up the phone and call 555-1313. That's my foreman, Junior. Tell him to bring the hands over here right now. We'll ride your uncle's horses home and get your cows. Mr. McElhanney has no bill of sale, then he has no legal right to the cows."

"You can't do this! I'll have you in prison."

"You can recoup your losses from Nate Peebles," Hank said as he pushed McElhanney into the wall hard enough to knock the breath out of him. "You weren't going to report the income on the cows, were you? A nice little tax dodge." He nodded as he talked. "I may just give a call to the IRS and see if they've audited you lately."

McElhanney caught his breath. "You are a downright bastard, Hank Dalton."

"You're a crook and a scoundrel. Now I wouldn't go any further with this name calling or I'm going to call you an empty colostomy bag and it's going to be true because I'm going to stomp the hell out of you."

McElhanney backed against the wall. Familiar leapt onto the filing cabinet next to him and hissed.

Hank turned to Stephanie, who was smiling. "Keep an eye on him. If he tries to use the phone, jerk it out of the wall. I'm going out to get the cows ready. We'll just drive them back home."

"Saddle a horse for me, if you get time," she said. "And where is Banjo?"

Hank turned to McElhanney. When he didn't speak, Hank reached out and grabbed his shirt again. "I can't tell you how long I've wanted to thump you into next Sunday. Please, please give me a reason."

"The dog is locked in a cage in the barn. He kept trying to go home."

Hank pushed McElhanney back against the wall, knocking the breath out of him again. "One word of disrespect to Ms. Chisholm, and I'll make you regret it the rest of your life. Got it?"

Familiar arched his back, fur puffed out and growled.

McElhanney cowered against the wall and nodded.

CIMARRON TROTTED up to the rear of the herd as Stephanie caught up with Hank. From behind, she couldn't help but admire his seat in the saddle. And his shoulders. And the way he used his body to control his horse.

He heard her horse and turned over his shoulder, a smile breaking out on his face. "How does it feel to be a cattle rustler?" he asked. He leaned back so he could address Familiar, who was reluctantly seated behind Stephanie on Cimarron's back. "Now I've seen a lot of things, but I've never seen a cat ride a horse."

"It feels wonderful to be back in the saddle, at least to me. Familiar isn't thrilled, but riding back was preferable to staying with Avis McElhanney, that creep."

"You look good in the saddle," Hank said, his gaze taking in her legs and posture.

"Cimarron is still as good a ride as she was two summers ago." Her smile faltered. "Uncle Albert bought her for my birthday. She's six now."

"I know she'll be glad to get home."

They both turned at the yipping of a dog. Banjo broke out of the ditch, herding a stray heifer. The dog sent the cow back to the herd, then changed directions and went after a calf that had strayed into someone's front yard.

"He's the best cow dog I've ever seen," Hank said.

"Uncle Albert adored him. He slept on the bed with

them." Stephanie held on to her smile. She had to get to the place where every good memory didn't bring pain. Uncle Albert and Aunt Em wouldn't want her to suffer for them. They'd want her to be happy, and she knew they'd be happy if they could see her moving cattle down County Road 17 and back to McCammon Ranch.

"Used to be every rancher in the county drove his herd to market like this," Hank said. "Now the roads are too busy. City folk don't like the inconvenience of traveling behind cows."

"City folk like me?" Stephanie asked. She felt his cool gaze assess her again.

"You don't look too refined this minute," he said. "You'd better check a mirror. You've got a streak of dirt down your right cheek and what looks to be, naw, couldn't be what I think it is, right by your right ear."

Stephanie put a hand up and felt the dirt and something else. Something that could be sweat or worse. She brushed it away. "Thanks, Hank. You're compliments are about as sweet as your disposition."

He was still laughing when she closed her legs on Cimarron and leapt forward to check on the front of the herd. They only had about two miles to go, and so far she hadn't heard any sirens coming after her. McElhanney must have been thoroughly cowed, no pun intended, not to call the police. She smiled. She'd won the first battle, but the war was far from over. Hank had told her about the dozer. As soon as she got back to the ranch, she was calling a towing company to move it. The owner could pay for the towing and the impound. That was what happened when someone trespassed on ranch property.

She saw the white fence post that marked the edge of the McCammon property. They'd made it. She looked behind her at the cows as they meandered on home. There wasn't any point to make them hurry. They were just happy to be away from the place where they smelled death.

She leaned forward in the saddle and asked Cimarron to gallop. The little quarter horse mare responded with a blaze of speed. Stephanie let out a whoop, and then remembered Familiar was right behind her. She reached back to steady him. "Sorry, fella," she said. "I just got carried away. This is my first cattle drive, and I just had a brainstorm. I could set up greenhorn drives. That way I'd never have to sell a single cow again."

Greenhorn cattle drive. Sounds like hell. Who in his right mind would want to sit on top of a horse for hours on end, pushing cattle from one place to the next. I can just imagine how it was in the glory days of the west. A bunch of old men, riding horses for days, no baths or showers unless they hit a creek or it rained, bad food, sleeping on the ground. Right. A dream come true. Not for this kitty. As soon as we get to the house, I'm going to get something to eat and recline on a soft bed. I think I'm getting saddle sore!

But I learned some interesting things today. Whoever is behind all of Stephanie's troubles is someone who can move fast and get things done. Nate Peebles. I think it's time we paid this lawyer a visit. If I can get a ride into town, I can do a bit of sleuthing on my own. Hank, it seems, will have his hands busy with Stephanie.

I've been watching the two of them. He's attracted to her, but just when it seems he's going to make a move, he backs away. Then he gets this stern look on his face. And when he mentioned her being a city girl, he wasn't teasing. There's something there, but I don't know what.

As to Stephanie, I think she's beginning to find joy in the life she once disdained. I know she was engaged to marry Johnny Benton before she left for New York City. She told me that her folks liked Johnny and sort of pushed him on her. She went along with it as long as she could. A few weeks before the wedding, she returned his ring and left for the city. She did her best to fulfill her aunt and uncle's dreams for her, but she had to have her own dream. Now, though, the pressure is off, and she's beginning to enjoy the ranch. And Hank.

Now, I wonder what kind of menu Stephanie is going to offer for my dinner tonight. I gave her my brochure, which lists all of my kitty needs: heavy cream, fresh salmon, something crunchy, any type of grilled seafood or chicken, catnip treats for when I need some herbal help, scratching post, clean litter on those days when I have to stay in and think. She's a great hostess—I'm looking forward to dinner.

HANK SAT BACK at the table and gazed at the faces of his cowhands and Rodney. They were replete and satisfied. Four of the men got up to go outside and smoke cigarettes, and the others followed. Finally he was alone with Stephanie. He stood up and began to help clear the table. Stephanie had surprised them all by putting out a spread that was as delicious as it was colorful.

"Where'd you learn to cook like that?" he asked as he helped her load the dishwasher.

"Aunt Em taught me a lot, and then I took some cooking classes in the city. Believe it or not, I entertained a lot. Advertising has a lot of wooing the client involved."

"What did you advertise?"

"All sorts of things. Brokerage firms, baseball teams, news programs. We did a lot of television."

"Did?" He'd heard her correctly, but he wasn't certain what tense she'd meant to use.

She turned to face him. "I may not go back."

He didn't bother to hide his surprise. "Really?"

"Is that so shocking?" She stepped past him so that her face was hidden from his view behind her dark curls. "I had an idea today. I need to investigate it before I talk about it, but I may be able to keep the ranch running."

"Want to bounce it off me?"

She turned to him, smiling. "We say that a lot in advertising where we try ideas out on one another."

"Ranching has gotten very sophisticated." He laughed. She was easy to talk to, and even though she had a fancy job in a big city, she didn't act like she thought she was better than others. And she looked so excited about the scheme she'd hatched. He couldn't help but wonder what her idea might be.

"Thank you for your help today, Hank. I don't know what I would have done without you."

"It wasn't anything." He wanted to reach out and pull her against him, but it would be completely inappropriate. He'd met her only that day, and Stephanie was a grown woman who knew her own mind. She wasn't the kind of woman to be attracted to a rancher.

"It was a lot. I don't know what I would have done. That creep would have killed the cows and both of us know it."

"He would have done his best to kill them." Hank leaned against the refrigerator. "Where in tarnation is that cat?"

"According to his contract—"

"Contract?" Hank asked. "You've got to be kidding."

"I told you, he's a legitimate detective. According to his contract, he's served grilled seafood or chicken. I made some snapper for him. He ate and now he's taking a snooze."

"He is something else. I think if McElhanney had made a move toward you he would have bitten his nose off."

"Or worse. I take a lot of comfort in Familiar. Now Banjo is home, too, so I'll be fine."

"If you're frightened, I can stay."

She walked up to him. "I've never had a man stay with me because I was frightened of anything. I won't start with you."

"I didn't mean—"

She put her fingers on his lips. "I know what you meant. I'm okay, Hank." She stood on tiptoe and kissed him lightly on the lips. "I'm really okay. I know how to shoot a gun, and believe me, I will."

"I'm going to block that trapdoor in your bedroom before I go."

She nodded. "That room was originally designed for a child back when the ranch house was built in the 1800s. I'd forgotten all about it. If you'll do that, I'll finish cleaning the kitchen."

Rodney had left the supplies in the bedroom, and it took Hank only a few minutes to hammer a board across the trap door. It wasn't the prettiest carpentry job he'd ever done, but it was effective. No one could sneak into the house.

While he was there, he took a quick look around to make sure no one was hiding in the extra bedrooms or closets. He found Familiar asleep on a down comforter in a guest bedroom. When he returned to the kitchen, Stephanie was running cold water into the coffeepot to set it up for the next day.

"I'll be going then."

She put the pot down and walked up to him. "Thanks."

Her lips were so inviting, turned up to him. He wasn't a man to pass an invitation like that. He bent down to kiss her, intending a light kiss. When she opened her mouth to accept his kiss, he pulled her tight against him. The kiss was as surprising as it was unexpected.

When she drew away from him, he released her, though his gaze lingered on her lips. He'd never felt such a dizzying array of emotions before. He touched her cheek, wanting to draw her back to him for another kiss. He was about to do just that when she spoke.

"Thank you, Hank. I'll ride over tomorrow and make sure my cows aren't causing any difficulty for you."

He'd been dismissed. "Yes, ma'am. If you're done with me, I guess I'll be heading home."

Chapter Four

Stephanie tapped the toe of her designer heel as she sat in the waiting room of Nate Peebles's office. It was ten o'clock, and she'd been waiting an hour. As aggravating as waiting was, it was more so because her thoughts kept slipping back to a tall rancher named Hank Dalton. She'd spent a restless night, tossing and turning, as if the fire of his kiss continued to heat her body. The kiss had been completely inappropriate. What in the world had possessed her? Sure, Hank was a generous man. So he'd come to her aid without any benefit to himself. It was true he was handsome and well mannered and had an easy charm. And even thinking about him now, she wanted to kiss him again. But for heaven's sake, he was a stranger.

It seemed that coming back to Texas had stirred a lot of emotions she'd worked hard to suppress. She had no desire to end up like some of her friends—being led around by her heart.

The secretary cleared her throat and gave Stephanie

a look. Stephanie picked up her purse and checked her makeup in a hand mirror. Peebles was testing her patience, and he was probably doing it deliberately. Far better to concentrate her irritation at the lawyer than to daydream about kissing Hank.

The door to Peebles's inner office swung open and a tall, well-dressed man stepped out. "Ms. Chisholm?" He raised his eyebrows as if there was some doubt. There was no one else in the room except his secretary.

She rose and walked past him. When he didn't close the door, she did so.

"Please have a seat," he offered.

She bent to examine the chair. "Oh, is this a chair you actually paid for? Or did you steal it from someone?"

A red flush covered his cheeks, and she felt a stab of satisfaction.

"I understand how you might be upset over the Mc-Cammon will, but throwing insults and tantrums won't change a legal document."

She glanced past him to the window. Familiar sat on the ledge, watching. The cat was uncanny in the way he always ended up being in the right place. "I'm going to do more than hurl a few insults, Mr. Peebles. I'm suing you." She smiled at the startled look on his face. "I'm not some local girl you've rooked out of her future. I retain a firm of lawyers in New York with contacts in every state. Prepare yourself for some serious litigation."

"Sue me for what?"

"False representation. I think the Texas bar would be interested in how my aunt and uncle dispersed their property, even though I have a will dated only six months ago which makes other provisions."

"People have a right to change their minds." He dropped all expression from his face. "Ms. Chisholm, you're wasting your time and mine. I have clients in ten minutes. It would be best if you left now."

"Absolutely," she said, walking to the door. "You'd better call that realtor and tell him to back off trying to sell the ranch until this is settled. And by the way, that dozer you sent out to tear out the fences has been impounded. I gave the tow truck operator your numbers."

She was pleased with the anger in his eyes. She wanted him to know right off the bat she wasn't going to roll over and pretend to go along with him. She left his private office, and the secretary virtually shooed her out the door. As soon as she was on the street, she hurried around to the side of the wooden building. Familiar was still on the ledge, and she slipped beside him, ducking behind a sweet-smelling gardenia when she thought Peebles was approaching the window. Instead of looking out, the lawyer picked up the telephone and began to talk with animation. Stephanie couldn't hear him, and she couldn't read his lips. She could only tell that he was greatly agitated. She was proud of the result of her five-minute visit with him.

"I'd give anything to know who he's talking to," she said aloud.

"Meow," Familiar agreed.

They left his law office and went to the county courthouse. Familiar slipped in with her, and in ten minutes she was in a vault going over probated wills. It took two hours—and Familiar's help—but she found three recent incidents where Nate Peebles had been named as a beneficiary in someone's will for significant amounts. He was listed in at least twenty others for small gifts. The man was using his law license to scam the elderly out of their belongings. She closed her book and folded her list to put in her pocket. Surely someone else had challenged the lawyer. Maybe a complaint had even been filed with the bar. She had grounds now for legal action.

It was lunchtime, and Stephanie walked down the streets of the small town headed for Main Street. At the end of town was the rodeo arena where the Friday night events were held. When she was in high school, it was the thing all the boys focused on. Riding the broncs or the bulls and roping. It was the measure of the man in Pecos, Texas.

Stephanie's problem was that she felt sorry for the stock. She'd ridden her little mare, Mirage, in the barrel racing and timed events competitions, along with the other girls. The horses, for the most part, were well treated. But the steers and broncs and bulls didn't always meet a happy fate, and it had dampened Stephanie's joy in watching the sports. Still, there had been a lot of good memories.

She was drawn to the arena, and she walked down the street toward it. Familiar was swatting at her ankles, trying to herd her in the direction of Maizy's Café, but she ignored him. Something was different about the arena. Something was wrong. When she realized what it was, she stopped in the middle of the street. A cowboy in a pickup honked his horn, then stopped and whistled at her. She ignored him and walked toward the abandoned arena in disbelief. They'd shut it down. The arena was the heart and soul of Pecos. What in the world had happened? Why hadn't Uncle Albert mentioned it to her?

The facility looked as if it hadn't been used in years, and she tried to remember, with no results, the last time she'd seen an event there. She stared at it until Familiar sank his claws into the top of her foot. "Okay, okay, already. We'll get lunch. But first." She pulled her cell phone out of her purse. The realty sign on the arena was the same one that had been at the ranch. She called the broker, Todd Hughes.

"I want to make an offer on the old arena." It would work out perfectly with her new plan for McCammon Ranch.

"You what?" the realtor asked.

"I'm offering ten thousand dollars." If she wanted to look at it like an optimist, she'd say this was the money she'd saved when she tried to buy the cows back. Having some cash in the bank was only one of the benefits of her successful business.

"Ms. Chisholm, in all fairness, I have to tell you that property isn't prime. So many of the ranches are being parceled off. There just isn't any need for a rodeo arena."

"I have a need for one."

The realtor sighed. "I'll tender your offer to the owner."

"Do it fast," Stephanie said. "And call me on my cell phone when you get an answer." She left the number. She was smiling when she looked down at the cat. "How about something seafood and grilled? I'm treating today."

HANK HAD BEEN up since dawn, and the midday heat had finally driven him into the ranch house for a shave, shower and some food. The cattle had migrated over to Twisty Creek, and it was a pleasure to watch them drinking and wading in the fast-flowing waters. He'd been given a reprieve from his water problem, for the moment. But this was no guarantee, he knew. Stephanie's grasp on McCammon Ranch was tenuous, at best. And even if she won out and got to keep the farm, he wasn't certain she'd allow him access to water.

But it wasn't the water situation that preyed on his mind when he thought about Stephanie. It was that kiss. What in the world had possessed him? There were plenty of young women dedicated to ranch life who would kiss him—and more. Why in tarnation had he wanted so badly to kiss a New York advertising executive? Sure, she sat a horse like a pro. She was as beautiful in jeans as a designer suit. She could cook like her aunt Em, and she had a kind, easy way with the ranch hands. The bottom line was that after a few months, she'd get bored with the ranch and head back to the city. He knew all about women like that. He'd suffered the effects of being left behind when his mother decided that law practice in Pecos wasn't challenging enough.

She liked the glamour and fast pace of Dallas, where she still lived.

That had been fine for her, but for the twelve-year-old son she'd left behind, the emotional devastation had been tough. Hank and his dad had been left to work the ranch. Jared Dalton had been a hard worker. Had, in fact, worked himself into an early grave. Hank had been unable to prevent it. He'd watched as his father killed himself making a go of a ranch his mother despised. So why had he kissed Stephanie? Why had he allowed himself to feel that surge of desire for her that he'd never felt for another woman? It was more than desire. A lot more. And that was what upset him. Best just to keep his distance from Stephanie. They'd run into each other; that was unavoidable. But he wouldn't allow himself to be alone with her. The wise strategy was to protect his heart and avoid temptation.

He finished his shave and shower and went to the kitchen. When he opened the refrigerator, he remembered that a week ago he'd needed to buy groceries. He slipped on his boots and hat and went to the truck. He could always get a good lunch at Maizy's, and the truth was, it was about as cost-effective as his cooking. Besides, he needed to run some other errands in town.

He drove for twenty minutes until he saw the outskirts of town. To his surprise, a couple of workers were removing the For Sale sign on the arena. For a second his heart jolted with hope. Pecos had been steadily going downhill since the rodeo had been closed down. But no one in his right mind would buy the arena. Housing developments were replacing the ranches where local high school kids learned the skills of ranching. The teenagers interested in learning to ranch couldn't afford to board a horse. A way of life was being lost, and there seemed little anyone could do about it. Probably the person who bought the arena was going to level it and build a Super Wal-Mart.

The lunch rush was over at Maizy's, a diner that offered plate menus and Texas barbecue. He walked in and stopped. Stephanie rose from her booth where she was sitting alone. Her smile was radiant. He was so caught by surprise that he smiled back at her. She looked like she'd just won the lottery.

"Hank! You're never going to believe it, but I just bought the old arena!"

A feather could have knocked him over. He tried to think of something to say, but no words would come to him.

Doubt crossed her face. "Don't you think it's a good idea?"

"What are you going to do with it?" he asked, still fighting to regain his balance.

"Have Friday night rodeos," she said, excited once again. "Only different. I've been really worried about how I was going to run the ranch and all of that without actually having to sell the cattle for butcher, and now I've figured it out. I saw the sale sign on the arena and it came to me in a flash."

Hank sank down into the booth, surprised to find the black cat beside him with a plate of grilled shrimp in front of him. The cat looked up and greeted him with a meow and then returned to his food. Hank needed to sit so he could fully focus on everything she was saying. He'd caught the edges of what she'd said about ranching without selling the cows, but he didn't understand. "What are you talking about?"

He knew his tone wasn't as enthusiastic as it might have been, but he was concerned. He saw her purse her lips as she thought it through. The waitress came and he placed his order for fried chicken.

"One of the biggest reasons I never wanted to stay on the ranch was the cows." He could see she was trying to phrase things with delicacy. "I hated it when Uncle Albert sold them. I hated hearing the babies crying when they were shipped off." She held up a hand. "I know it's the business. Believe me, I understand that ranchers raise cattle for butcher. I'm not judging it, I'm just saying it really bothered me."

"Stephanie, a ranch can't make it if the cattle aren't sold, and sold for a profit. Some of the herd is sold for breeding stock, but the majority goes for meat."

"I know that. I'm not arguing with you. But I have an idea where it wouldn't have to be that way."

The joy in her face was more than enough to convince him that maybe she could make it work. Good god, he wanted it to work for her. He realized with a pang of desperation that if Stephanie Chisholm told him she was going to fly cows to the moon, he'd try to help her.

"I'm going to start city slicker cattle drives, just like

we did the other day. We can just push the cows around the ranch, or maybe you'd let us use some of your land, too, for rights to Twisty Creek—" she lifted her eyebrows in a hopeful arch "—and I'm going to have a rodeo school. Where young people can learn the skills of the cowboy. I can make sure all the stock is taken care of properly. They won't ever have to be shipped or transported. They can just come in off the pastures and work Friday nights and then go home."

Hank felt the smile spread over his face. He reached across the table and took her hands. "Stephanie, it's brilliant!" He couldn't believe it. She'd been back in town less than two days and had seen the problems Pecos faced and come up with a solution. She was amazing.

"Hank, we can make this work. I know we can. If the animals are well treated, I love the idea of a rodeo. And the ranch house is big enough to accommodate at least fifteen guests for the cattle drive. We could do thirty a year, ending with the Friday night rodeos."

She was so alive and so filled with her plans that he simply wanted to stare at her. He'd never seen a woman so animated, so full of passion. "It was the cattle that made you leave Pecos?" he asked.

She took a deep breath. "I just couldn't do it another spring. No rancher can afford to feed an entire herd over the summer with the chances of drought. Uncle Albert loved his cattle. He did. He gave them a terrific life as long as he had them, but I just couldn't go through another spring sale. I had to leave." She shrugged. "I wanted to try my hand at advertising, so I went to New York."

"Stephanie, if you decide to follow through on your plans, you won't be able to live in New York." He tried not to put any emphasis on his observation. Stephanie was a woman who had to make up her own mind. Even though he wanted her to say she was staying in Pecos, he couldn't press her into it.

"I won't worry about that today," she said. She squeezed his hand. "First, I have to make sure I get the ranch. I stopped by for a visit with Nate Peebles today, and he's clinging to his version of the will like a rat terrier."

"Where do you stand legally?"

"That's what we're about to find out." She bent closer to tell him what she'd discovered in the courthouse.

When he sat back, he realized the cat was staring at him. "I think Peebles may be behind a lot of the problems you've been having," Hank said. Edging back from the table, Hank made room for the waitress to serve his food.

"I agree. The question is what to do about it."

"I have a plan," Stephanie said, and from the smile on her face, he knew he wanted to hear it.

Chapter Five

Hank sat at his desk and stared at the telephone. The sun was slipping behind the tree line to the west, and still he couldn't force himself to pick up the receiver. He was torn between his desire to help Stephanie and his unwillingness to ask his mother for a single thing. She'd left him. She'd made her choice that the law was more important than family long ago. If she'd wanted to help him, she would have stayed and been his mother.

On the other hand, Stephanie was getting in way over her head. If it turned out that the will which named Nate Peebles the beneficiary of the McCammon estate was ruled valid, then Stephanie was going to lose out in more ways than one.

"Damn." He picked up the phone and dialed the number of his mother's house in Dallas. He knew it by heart, though he never called her. Their relationship, at his insistence, consisted of Christmas cards.

"Lorry Dalton," she answered.

Hank cleared his throat. "Mother, it's me."

There was a pause. "Hank, is something wrong?"

For a split second he hated the fact that the sound of his voice made her worry. But what else could she expect? The last time he'd called her was to tell her Jared had died of a heart attack. "I need some advice," he said.

There was the sound of her breathing deeply. "Of course, whatever I can do to help."

He launched into the details of Stephanie's problems. When he finished, his mother asked, "Have you seen this alleged will?"

"Not yet."

"They'll have to hold a formal reading. Your friend should have her legal ducks in a row there and be prepared to protest the will."

"She can do that."

"The evidence that this Peebles person is acting illegally is strong if he's named as a beneficiary in a number of wills. It would behoove Stephanie to have these families lined up and ready to testify in her behalf if it becomes necessary."

Hank added that to the list he was making.

"Who is this woman, Hank?"

The question hung there. "She's my neighbor. She has water and I don't."

"Is it that simple?"

The question infuriated him. Who was Lorry Dalton to act as if she had a right to ask him personal questions?

"This is none of your business."

"I'm sorry," she said. "I'd ask the same of a client."

The pang that hit him only made him angrier. First,

he didn't want her to ask personal questions, and then when she informed him it wasn't personal, he was mad about that. "Forget it. She's Albert and Emily McCammon's niece."

"The young girl they took in after her parents divorced."

"That's her."

"I remember her as a child. She was lovely. Dark, curly hair, and she could ride anything with four legs."

"That's her."

"I remember once when your father and I were there for dinner. She'd just come there to live. She threw a fit, saying she was going to be a vegetarian. It was the most startling thing to hear on a cattle ranch."

Hank could well imagine it, and the image made him smile. "She hasn't changed a bit." He realized too late how much he'd given away by his tone of voice.

"If Ms. Chisholm wins the rights to the ranch, do you suppose she'll run cattle?"

"She has a plan." Hank didn't want to go into details. "Mother, I'm worried. Stephanie has decided to stay at the ranch. Alone. She believes she can draw Peebles into some kind of threatening behavior."

"Not a good idea."

"I told her that. She's stubborn."

His mother's laugh was as light and musical as he remembered. "Now that's the pot calling the kettle black."

"Right." He wasn't amused. "Is there some legal action I can take to help ensure her safety?"

"You can call the sheriff and tell him your suspicions. That will alert him, and if something untoward should happen and Stephanie is forced to act to protect herself, it will go a long way toward showing that she had cause to take action. One word of caution, Hank. I learned the hard way that often there's a good ole boys club in small towns. Stephanie doesn't belong. Help from the sheriff may be predicated on belonging."

Hank was concerned. "She's going to publicly confront this guy. In town. At the courthouse. Tomorrow."

"Can you stop her?"

"I don't know."

"Hank, if this lawyer is hooked up, he and his friends will go to extremes to keep from being exposed."

"What should I do?"

"If it were me, and I was in love with this woman, I'd do whatever it required to keep her from being hurt."

For all the time they'd been apart and the distance that he'd kept her at, his mother was a very perceptive woman. "What makes you think I love her?" he asked.

"You haven't called me, voluntarily, in ten years. I don't think a little concern on behalf of your new neighbor would suffice to make you call today. I can only imagine that Stephanie Chisholm is some kind of woman."

"She is."

"I'll do a little research into the law regarding wills. I'll get back with you when I have something."

"Thanks, Mom."

STEPHANIE WENT TO THE WALL safe and removed the will again. Unfolding and reading as she walked, she went into the kitchen where she'd made herself a glass of iced tea. The will was dated for November of the past year. Six months ago. How, or why, had her uncle signed an entirely new will? It didn't make a lick of sense, especially since he'd always made his intentions clear regarding McCammon Ranch. He'd talked about it, even when she was a child. Aunt Em had been in complete agreement that the ranch would be made into a trust, with Stephanie the administrator. They had both been adamant that Stephanie would always have a home on the ranch, if she chose to live there.

She put the will away and sat down at the kitchen table to think. Looking out the window, she saw the black cat sitting in the yard, watching the barn. It would be nice to take a ride, maybe go out and check on the cows. She'd loved doing that with her uncle. It would be good to give Mirage a little exercise, too. She'd just put her empty glass in the sink when she heard the doorbell ringing. Who in the world would come to visit now?

She went to the front door and opened it to find Jackie and Johnny Benton standing there, a tray of foil-covered dishes in Jackie's hands.

"So many people brought food after the funeral," Jackie said, extending the tray. "They didn't know you would be in town. Neither did we. Everyone just ended up at our house."

Stephanie looked at the tray of food and felt her stomach churn. Food was the last thing she was interested in, but she realized that Johnny Benton might be able to help clear up some questions for her.

"Johnny, Jackie, come in," she said, holding the door open wide so they could enter with the food. "I'll make some coffee."

As soon as they were in the living room, she took the tray and went to the kitchen. She put everything down and started the coffeepot, calming her volatile emotions as she worked. The Bentons were trying to be neighborly. Bringing funeral food was a kind thing to do, and in their own way, they were trying to show her that she was part of the community. Of course, the result was just the opposite—they only made her feel more of an outsider. But that wasn't their intention.

She went back to the living room and took a seat in a wing chair opposite the sofa where they sat. "It was nice of you to bring the food." She felt more than awkward. She'd dated Johnny Benton for almost a year and had almost married him.

"Johnny told me all about your engagement," Jackie said, as if she could read Stephanie's discomfort. "I know this isn't easy, but I want us all to be friends. Everything happens for a reason, and if you'd married Johnny, I wouldn't have had a chance." She smiled. "We're very happy."

"That's wonderful." Stephanie forced a smile. The glance she cast at Johnny Benton let her know that he wasn't paying a bit of attention to his wife. He was too busy studying her. "I'll check on that coffee." She escaped from the room and took as long as possible preparing a tray of coffee, cream and sugar. When she headed back to the living room, she'd steeled herself to endure the visit. No matter what off-the-wall thing Jackie said, Stephanie wasn't going to react.

She served the coffee and sat down with a cup of black. "I gather you were close with Uncle Albert and Aunt Em," she said to Johnny. "When did you see them last?"

"About two weeks before they were killed," he said. A sad smile touched his lips. "Albert was in the pink of health. Em, too. They were both living life to the fullest. The accident was just so unexpected."

"Yes," Stephanie said, feeling the sudden pressure of tears. She couldn't afford to cry, though. She had to find out what had happened to her relatives. "What were they doing out in the barn, do you know?"

"Albert had been talking about remodeling that barn to make some living quarters for some of the hands. He was thinking of an apartment, with a kitchen and all. That way the person living there could have all the amenities of a home."

Stephanie lifted her eyebrows. Rodney had said Albert was working on an old tractor. "An apartment sounds smart. It would also give him someone on the property twenty-four hours a day if he and Aunt Em ever decided to take that vacation they talked about for the past thirty years."

"That's exactly what he said." Johnny smiled. "He was a planner, your uncle was."

"He and Aunt Em were happy, right?" Stephanie asked.

"They were very happy. They missed you, but they talked about you all the time, about how you were doing so well. They were proud of you."

She'd heard that from several people, and it only served to make her feel more guilty. She turned to Jackie. "You must have spent a good bit of time with Aunt Em."

"I did," Jackie said. "She taught me so much."

"Em sure improved her cooking," Johnny said.

"Oh, go on with you!" Jackie slapped his arm lightly with her fingertips. "It's true, though, Em taught me a lot, including cooking."

"Did Uncle Albert ever talk about how he wanted the ranch to be, after he died?" It wasn't a subtle approach, but the Bentons might make good witnesses for her defense.

"For a long time he talked about some kind of trust, where the ranch would always be a working ranch. Lately, though, he was sort of disheartened. He felt the ranching life was a thing of the past." Johnny stared at his boots.

"Stephanie, I don't want to be cruel, but Emily and Albert were worn slap out. They felt since you'd made it clear you didn't want to ranch…" Jackie faded to silence at the glare from her husband.

Stephanie hoped her feelings didn't show on her face. She was devastated. It was bad enough to think her uncle had lost the taste for a life he'd loved, but it was worse to think he hadn't felt that he could rely on her.

Jackie fidgeted on the sofa. "Anyway, last winter, I guess it was, the cold was just too much for Albert. He said something about getting rid of the ranch." She shrugged one shoulder. "It wasn't my place to press him on it, so I didn't get any details."

Johnny stood up. "Come on, Jackie, we've got a lot to do at home."

When Stephanie rose, he put his arms around her and drew her into a hug. Her first instinct was to brace herself and resist. Then she reminded herself Johnny Benton was long over her. He was happily married and moving on with his life, as she should do. She allowed him to hug her and then stepped back.

"Thank you both for coming, and thank you for taking time to be with Uncle Albert and Aunt Em."

Johnny nodded. "I always felt they were family."

"What are you going to do with the ranch?" Jackie asked. "Talk in town is that you had a For Sale sign on it before the funeral was over, but I didn't see a sign."

Stephanie bit her tongue and held back the sharp reply. "I'm not certain what will happen." She didn't know either of them well enough to confide her plans, but she couldn't help adding, "It sure is wonderful to be home again, though. Especially since I've worked through my issues with raising cattle." She saw the startled look on Johnny's face.

"I know you were always bothered by selling the cows."

"That's true, but I have an idea. So how is your ranch?" she asked, turning the conversation. Johnny had worked on the Betty June Ranch and had inherited it when old man Clay had gotten ill and had to be put in a nursing home.

"Ranching isn't the life it used to be," Johnny said. "The Betty June isn't large enough to support enough cattle to operate strictly as a ranch. Jackie and I are thinking about some diversification."

"What kind of diversification?" Stephanie felt a dull thud of doom. The Betty June bordered McCammon Ranch to the east. Whatever Johnny did with his land could easily impact hers.

"We're thinking of maybe selling out," Jackie said. "Johnny has an offer in Austin to run a restaurant and bar."

Stephanie didn't know how to respond. "I'm sorry," she said. "I know how hard you've worked on the Betty June."

"We'd best get going," Johnny said. He put his hat on and his hand on his wife's back as he assisted her to the door. "Don't be a stranger, Stephanie. Stop by and have a meal with us. Any night will do. No notice needed."

"Thanks," Stephanie said as she closed the door and leaned heavily against it. Had she bitten off more than she could chew? If a dedicated rancher like Johnny couldn't make it, could she?

Stephanie's old flame is leaving with his wife. Good. There's something I want Stephanie to see out here at this collapsed barn. It's for her eyes and hers alone. I made sure Rodney is gone from the barn, where he seems to hang out-all the time. It was a simple matter of opening a few stall doors and sending the little mares out for a free run. It'll take him at least half an hour to round up all six horses. Now I have to get Stephanie.

A little body slam against the front door and here she is, looking down at me with a really tired look on her face. She's worried, and what I have to show her isn't going to help.

She's reluctant to follow me, but a few sharp claws in the old calf is enough. I have to say as attractive as cowboy boots are, they make it difficult for me to get the necessary attention. I have to really stretch to get my claws in a bit of flesh. But it's done. We're outside, and though I see by her face she knows where we're going, I have to insist.

The tractor barn is some three hundred yards from the house. From the medical documents I saw on the deaths of Albert and Emily, they were killed at approximately one-thirty in the afternoon. That would be right after lunch. I have to recreate their day. Anything out of the abnormal is fodder for consideration.

Now it hasn't been easy, but from hanging around outside and listening to some of the other hands talk, Emily served a bodacious lunch every day to all three of the full-time wranglers. Rodney is the only one left, and he seems to have it made. Apparently the renovation of the old barn was a project designed for Rodney and his fiancée, soon to be his wife. The two of them were to move into the apartment. He's still living in the bachelor quarters in the horse barn, which is the same distance from the house, a little to the east of the tractor barn.

Stephanie is slowing down. I need to motivate her a little more. She has to see what I've discovered. Someone has cleaned up a good bit of the debris, but the support beams are obviously sunk deep into the ground. It makes me wonder if that heavy equipment Hank found was really sent here to take out the fences or to bulldoze the rest of the barn into the dirt. That would certainly destroy all the evidence.

Here we are, at last. Stephanie is hanging back, but I'll just trot over to this support beam. I'll give her a little kitty call, and here she comes, picking her way through the fallen lumber and debris that's left. Someone got most of the wood and the hay out of the way already, which made it easier for me to find this.

She's bending down where I'm showing her. She sees it. Her fingers are tracing over the rough cut on the beam. It's almost at ground level. And here's another one. And another. I found eight beams in all that looked as if they'd been deliberately weakened.

I don't doubt that the barn fell on top of Emily and Albert and killed them, but it wasn't a wind shear that brought it down. I'd be willing to bet someone hooked a tractor to the barn and pulled it down after it had been structurally weakened.

No doubt now, this is a murder investigation.

Chapter Six

Hank did a one-eighty in the gravel in front of the ranch house. Stephanie had sounded terrible on the phone, like she'd lost all of her life and spunk. It was the deadness of her tone that terrified him. He'd driven like a maniac, and now that he was at the ranch house, he wasn't certain where to look for her. She'd called from her cell phone.

He thought about what she'd said, and he realized the clue was in her words. She'd said that she knew for certain now that Albert and Emily had been murdered. He jumped out of his truck and ran toward the old barn that had collapsed. Sure enough, he saw her standing in front of what was left of the old barn, the black cat at her feet, Banjo standing on her other side. It was a sight that tore at his heart. He could only imagine what she was thinking. It was bad enough to lose someone you loved, but to have them murdered—that was unthinkable.

"Stephanie." He called her name softly as he approached. She was so still, he didn't want to startle her.

Not much chance of that with the cat, though. The feline had been watching him since he arrived. If it was possible, the cat seemed more sensitive than Banjo, who greeted him with a wagging tail.

"Hank," she said, still gripping the cell phone in her hand. "I'm sorry. I know I sounded like I'd lost it." She sighed and he saw the shimmer of tears in her eyes. "Familiar found something. I guess I just didn't want to believe anyone would hurt Uncle Albert and Aunt Em. But someone did."

She started walking into the rubble and he followed her. He'd seen the barn after it collapsed, but he hadn't examined it. Murder hadn't occurred to him at the time.

Stephanie pointed to a place where a huge support beam had been. There was the sign that someone had been digging in the spot. Hank knelt down and brushed some of the dirt away to reveal the stump of the support beam. He could feel across the surface of the beam that it had been cut. He took a deep breath and tried to compose his thoughts, because the first thing that came to his mind was revenge. When he had a grip on himself, he looked up at her. The grief and sorrow on her face were almost his undoing.

"It's been sawed, hasn't it?" Her lips were compressed.

"Yes," he said. "I'll check the others." He turned and looked around. "Where's Rodney?"

"I think Familiar let his horses out. He's chasing them down."

"Good. I think we should keep this between ourselves."

"You think Rodney—"

He could see by the expression on her face that she didn't want to believe the ranch hand was involved. "I don't think anything for certain. I just want to keep this between us. The less people who know, the more chances we'll have of flushing out the bast—man who did this."

She nodded. "I just can't believe this. I mean, I suspected, but I guess deep in my heart, I was hoping I would discover I was wrong. That a wind shear had knocked the barn down."

Hank didn't know what to say. He'd always been a man more comfortable with action than words, so he stepped up to her and put his arm around her shoulders. "I'm sorry."

She swallowed. "Me, too, but I vow to you whoever did this is going to be much, much sorrier than he ever dreamed." She glanced behind her. "No one will touch anything else here. We'll have time to look for more evidence. And where is the tractor? Rodney said Uncle Albert was repairing a tractor, but Johnny Benton said he and Aunt Em were thinking about building an apartment in the barn. One of the hands was getting married."

"Not Rodney," Hank said. "At least if it's him, he's kept it a big secret from everyone."

"I don't think that matters, but I do wonder where the tractor got off to."

"I'll check some of the tractor sales places," Hank said. "I'm beginning to believe that whoever did this had planned to have the whole ranch broken down and sold before you got home from New York."

"I think they've vastly underestimated me," Stephanie said.

Hank smiled because at last she was sounding like the woman he'd begun to fall for.

STEPHANIE TURNED on the coffeepot and opened the back door to the sunroom so she could watch for Rodney when he came back with the horses. Familiar sat on the counter with her. The plan was for her to divert Rodney so that Hank could have more time to examine the barn before dark fell.

If she looked out the kitchen window, she could see where the old barn had once stood. She could make out Hank's silhouette as he moved part of the roof and paced off the distance between the support beams. She'd taken him the digital camera she'd brought from the city, and once the photos were taken, they'd have some evidence.

Evidence of the murder of her family.

Beneath the threat of tears were cold fury and a wicked desire for revenge. Someone would pay. She made the silent vow to her aunt and uncle as she gripped the edge of the sink and watched Hank squat down and take a photo.

There wasn't time for self-pity, or even fury. She saw a cloud of dust coming from the east and hurried out the door to let Hank know Rodney was back and to draw the cowboy into the house so he was out of the way.

She ran across the yard and stopped, caught by the

sight of the wrangler coming across the wide pasture with five horses running in front of him. It was a picture that had defined Texas for a hundred years, and without a lot of help and protection, it would soon vanish. This was something she could help preserve, and she knew instantly that her instincts were right. She would fight for this, for a way of life Uncle Albert and Aunt Em loved and struggled to maintain. She would do this thing and neither hell nor high water would stop her. McCammon blood flowed in her veins, and she would not let some shyster lawyer destroy what her relatives had taken five generations to build.

She waved her arms and Rodney drew up short, the horses galloping by her with dust flying in all directions. The horses headed straight for the barn, each one running into its stall. She smiled up at the wrangler. "I need some help in the kitchen, if you don't mind."

"Not a bit. I'm just perplexed at how those horses got out of the barn, though. I mighta forgot to lock one stall door, but not every single one of them." He took off his hat and rubbed his forearm on his forehead. "I've pondered and pondered how that mighta happened, and I can't come up with anything."

Stephanie shook her head. "Remember when Albert's horse, Bandit, used to unlock all the stalls and then the pastures. It was mayhem."

Rodney's eyes brightened. "I sure do. I'd forgotten all about old Bandit. He lived to be thirty-three, and when he died, all the hands just about had to be shot."

Stephanie had been fourteen when Bandit had died.

Uncle Albert had been inconsolable, even though he hadn't ridden the horse for ten years. Bandit had been his friend. "I remember," she said. "I remember a lot of good memories here, Rodney."

They walked toward the barn and while he unsaddled Flicker, Stephanie latched the rest of the stall doors and made sure the horses had water and hay. Together she and Rodney walked back to the house. The wrangler never even cast a glance at the old barn where Hank waited behind a fallen gable.

Once in the kitchen, Stephanie poured Rodney a cup of coffee. "Have a seat before we get busy. It's been a long day."

"Sure has. I rode out to check on the cows. That bull dozer is gone."

Stephanie nodded. "I had it removed. The owner can find it impounded."

Rodney's eyes widened. "You sure know how to get things done, Miss Stephanie."

"City life has taught me some valuable lessons. Things I couldn't learn here. But I can sure apply them here. I know my rights, and I know how to protect what I love."

He nodded. "What can I do to help?"

"Think back to everyone who came to visit Aunt Em or Uncle Albert in the last month before they were killed." She watched his face closely. It was almost impossible to believe that Rodney was aligned with the forces trying to take McCammon Ranch. He'd been

Albert's head wrangler for the last ten years, and he'd worked on the ranch for several years before that.

"Let me see. Johnny and Jackie were here a good bit. They took a real interest in Albert and Em."

He didn't look at Stephanie; he didn't have to. She knew that neighbors had taken the place of family, and it hurt.

"Then there were the Smiths and Tanners. They came to visit last Sunday after church. And that Todd Hughes fellow. He was out a few weeks ago."

Stephanie had to bite down on her reaction. "He was? I wonder what he was doing here?"

"I think the Bentons sent him over. They were thinking about selling their place and I guess they thought Albert might want to sell, too."

That wasn't new information, but it was the perfect opportunity to test Rodney's attitude. "What did Uncle Albert say?"

"Not no, but hell no." Rodney grinned. "When Mr. Hughes realized that all of his statistics and figures on profit and investment opportunities weren't going to change Albert's mind, he went on home."

The irony was that not two weeks later, Albert and Em were dead and Hughes had the property up for sale. "You're sure Johnny sent him?"

Rodney shook his head. "Not really sure. That's just an assumption, but it coulda been anyone, really."

Anyone like Nate Peebles, Stephanie thought. She got the coffeepot and refilled his cup. "Have you or the other wranglers noticed anything unusual?" she asked.

He frowned as he concentrated. "Not really, unless you want to count the fact that Em was crying the morning they died."

"Crying?" Stephanie couldn't believe how painful it was to hear that her aunt was upset. "About what?"

"She never said. Albert sent me up to the house to get a pair of work gloves, and I guess I slipped up on Em. She was standing at the sink, looking out, crying."

"She didn't say about what?"

"Not to me. She acted embarrassed, and she kind of wiped the tears away and got the gloves. I guess I was embarrassed, too, so I acted like I didn't notice."

"Anything else?"

"Albert was sort of quiet that morning." He rubbed his forehead. "Fact is, he hardly said a word. He was intent on getting that tractor running, and he did."

Stephanie had a question about the tractor, but it could wait. "I heard in town that Albert was going to remodel the barn into some apartment."

Rodney's face brightened. "He was? Now that sounds just like him. He never said a word to me."

"I hear you're getting married," Stephanie said, watching his reaction. He turned red up to his ears.

"In a few months. Or maybe years. A man doesn't like to rush into such things."

"How long have you been seeing this woman?" She knew Rodney had to be at least forty-five.

"About two years."

She couldn't help the laughter that burst out. "I hardly think you're rushing things."

"Maybe not from your viewpoint, but I've had a mighty good life here. I've got my horses and the cows and Banjo. I'm not so sure I need to cram another single thing in there."

She laughed again. "Spoken like a true cowboy."

"You think I'm making a mistake?" he asked, and he was so sincere that Stephanie decided not to tease him.

"I think if you love this woman you should marry her. If you've gotten along for two years, I seriously doubt you'll discover you can't abide her."

Rodney smiled. "Em said exactly the same thing."

"I only wish I'd been here to hear it," Stephanie said. She poured herself a cup of coffee and sat across from him. "Rodney, do you know of anyone who wanted to hurt them?"

"No, ma'am. I can't think of a soul. Folks took to your aunt and uncle. They were kind and folks appreciated that."

Except for the obvious fact that someone had hurt them. "Did you know any of the people who were working on the old barn?"

"I never saw anyone there except Albert or one of the hands who went to get the tractor or some piece of equipment stored there. He didn't tell me anything about renovating it."

"Did you ever hear anyone working there?"

Rodney frowned. "As a matter of fact, there was one night I went to town and meant to stay with Wanda Nell, but I came home instead. There was someone working in there with a saw that night. When I went out to check, no one was there. I figured it was Albert finishing up some project."

"Did he go down there often?"

"Come to think of it, he didn't."

"Can you think of what night it was?"

"I don't remember, but I'll ask Wanda. She'll remember for sure. She's got a memory like an elephant, and she doesn't forget a thing."

"That would be a big help." Stephanie felt as if she'd gotten her first lead. "A big help. Do you know where all the other hands went?"

He looked a little sheepish. "They didn't want to leave, but most of them have children and they just didn't have a choice. They had to find work."

"I understand." She did. Economics were a hard fact of life. A man with a family had to have an income.

"I sure wish your aunt and uncle could see you today, Miss Stephanie. You're everything they ever bragged about."

It was a heartfelt compliment, and one that made her want to cry.

HANK TOSSED THE BOARD onto the pile of rubble. There was no doubt someone had tampered with the structural safety of the old barn. A slow fury burned through him as he thought about Albert and Emily, two people who'd always gone out of their way to help others.

Why would someone kill them?

It was a question with an obvious answer. Money.

Who would profit from their deaths? That was something he intended to find out.

He hadn't told Stephanie all he knew of Nate Peebles. The man had a serious gambling problem. He was a regular at the casinos in Las Vegas and the Mississippi Gulf Coast.

The cat crept out from under a pile of rubble, dust and cobwebs in his black coat. Familiar. He looked like the Halloween image of a witch's cat. And there was something extraordinary about him. Just like the woman who'd hired him.

"Meow." Familiar walked to a timber that was at least a foot square. He began to scratch on it.

Hank walked over to take a look and noticed the initials carved into it. S.C. Stephanie Chisholm. The wood had split just above that. He was about to turn away when he cat meowed again. He looked down at the glove that Familiar had unearthed. It was a common work glove, stained leather and worn fingers. He picked it up and decided to hold on to it. Just in case.

He tucked the glove into his back pocket and headed to the house, Familiar leaping at his side and Banjo barking and running in circles. For a split second Hank felt as if he were going home.

Chapter Seven

Hank and Stephanie had compared their findings and a comfortable silence had settled over the kitchen. Familiar took the last bite of his free-range chicken, and replete, yawned as he left the table. Stephanie watched him curl up on the sofa and fall asleep in the sunroom.

Hank shifted in his chair at the table, and Stephanie walked beside him, the coffeepot in her hand. From the kitchen window she could see the pastures of McCammon Ranch. How abruptly her life had changed. Two weeks ago she would have been having drinks in some swank restaurant with a client, pushing to close a deal before the sun disappeared below the New York skyline. Now, she was serving coffee to a rancher, both of them with a layer of dust on their boots. She poured the coffee and felt the pleasurable ache of muscles along her back and arms. No gym workout could give the sense of satisfaction that came from working on the land.

"Penny for your thoughts," Hank said, and she realized he was staring at her.

"Haven't you heard? Inflation. It'll cost at least a quarter."

He reached into his pocket and placed a coin on the table. "I've anted up so now you have to spill it."

She felt the warmth of a flush touch her cheeks. "I was thinking about how much satisfaction I find in working on the ranch." She could tell her answer surprised him.

"It wasn't the work that drove me away," she said softly. "Never the work. I just couldn't deal with watching the cows shipped off every year. I grew to dread it to the point that I had to leave."

"Would you have married Johnny Benton otherwise?"

She dropped her gaze from his. She'd thought about this often, and with a great degree of shame and regret. "No. I didn't love Johnny. Uncle Albert and Aunt Em wanted me to love him, so I thought I could."

"But you said yes when he asked you to marry him?"

Instead of getting angry, she felt only sadness. "I was eighteen at the time. High school was over. I wanted to go to college, but every time I brought it up, Aunt Em discouraged me. She wanted me to step into her shoes, and I think she was afraid if I got off to school I'd find other interests."

"That happened anyway."

"It was inevitable. But she only wanted my happiness. She and Uncle Albert thought they could protect me by keeping me here."

Hank picked up her hand and held it, examining the new blister she'd acquired while driving the cows. "You've forgiven them?"

"There was nothing to forgive. They did their best. I did what I had to do. My only regret is that I didn't come home more often. There are so many things about the ranch that I love. I think maybe I was afraid to come home. Afraid that I'd never be able to leave again."

She saw her words were affecting him, but she didn't understand why. She withdrew her hand. "Our families are just human, Hank. They do the best they can."

"I don't believe I can agree with you there." His face closed and the softness left his lips.

"So, tell me what you dream for the Running Z." She sat down, her hand still in his. She liked his touch. His hands were rough, work worn, but so tender. When he started to talk about his ranch, his face came alive again. He was a man as invested in his ranch as Uncle Albert had been in McCammon Ranch.

"I love ranching. I love the horses, the cows, Biscuit, just all of it. I'd like to keep a working ranch, if possible, but I have some problems with my water supply." He told her about the development and the ruinous results on Twisty Creek.

"Have you spoken to a lawyer?" she asked.

"Yes, but I don't want a lawsuit or money, I want a free-running creek for my herd to drink out of."

She could see how determined he was. "You're welcome to the water on my place as long as you need it." She gave a grim smile. "Or at least as long as I own it."

"We're going to get this figured out," Hank said.

She could have kissed him for including himself in her

troubles. In fact, his lips were so very inviting. She leaned forward slightly, and he met her more than halfway.

His kiss was firm, possessive. His hands moved over her back, encouraging her to move closer. She shifted and in a moment was in his lap. He smelled of dust and sun and horses. The scent of summer hay was in his hair, and she tightened her fingers into his dark curls and gave in to the sensations he aroused in her.

How long had it been since a kiss had affected her so? She couldn't remember. She'd dated a lot, and had found handsome and interesting men all over the city. But Hank was rock solid, his body a lean mass of muscle and heat. He made her feel excited and lethargic, all at once. He was so strong, and for the space of one kiss, she could allow herself not to be. It was the best luxury in the world, to let Hank hold her.

At last he broke the kiss. For a long moment he held her, nuzzled against his neck, as they both thought of their options. If he asked her to bed, she would go. If he didn't, she knew she would be disappointed, but also relieved.

"I haven't ever kissed a woman like that," he said, his hand stroking her hair.

"I know," she said. "It's a little frightening."

He shifted her in his arms so he could look at her. "You're not some kind of witch, are you?"

She smiled. "No one has ever asked me that question."

"I think you cast a spell on me." There was only a hint of worry in his eyes. "What would happen if I fell in love with you and you up and took off for New York City?"

"There aren't any guarantees," she said, understanding that she could offer no assurances, even if she wanted to.

"I saw what happened to my father after Mother left. It took his spirit. It broke him. I don't want to live through that, Stephanie."

She didn't want to hurt him, either. Hank wasn't a man who engaged in physical unions without also engaging his feelings. She was surprised, and excited. "Maybe we should back off this a little until we both know where we're headed." She slipped from his lap, leaned down and kissed him on the cheek. "That was one helluva kiss, Hank Dalton. I'll walk you to the door."

HANK WATCHED THE GLOW of a dozen fireflies as he sat on the porch at the Running Z. The ranch was quiet. Off in the distance he heard the occasional low of a cow, and farther away, the cry of a whippoorwill. All told, it was a quiet night, though. Most of the cows had calved, but there were still one or two waiting to deliver. It worried him. It might mean something was wrong with the calf or the mother, so he listened hard for the sound of an animal in distress. There was only the whippoorwill.

No matter how hard he fought it, his thoughts drifted again and again to Stephanie Chisholm. Her kiss had seared itself on his brain, and his heart. It had been magical, the sensation that his father had told him meant that rare thing—true love. He could see that he admired her. She was determined and honorable, and though she tried to hide it, she had a heart as big as Texas, and a tender one at that. He couldn't help but smile at the idea that she'd given up ranching because of her tender heart. He hated to admit it, but he sort of admired her. It was hard on everyone to sell the cattle, and if she could figure a plan where she didn't have to, then more power to her. She had something that a lot of cattle ranchers needed—the ability to think outside the box. She came at the business from a whole other direction, and she might have come up with a solution.

Cattle drives. He laughed softly at the idea. It might be fun to take a bunch of greenhorns and teach them to push cattle. It was certainly a part of the Old West that had disappeared. With eighteen-wheelers and refrigerator trucks, cattle drives were a thing of the past. But it might be fun to bring history to life again.

And the idea of a rodeo school was brilliant. The Friday night rodeo had closed in Pecos over four years before. The life had seemed to go out of the town then. If Stephanie could bring that back, with whatever humane rules she might want to establish, folks would get behind her.

But it all hinged on whether she kept McCammon Ranch or not. It wasn't hard to figure out that Nate Peebles had pulled something crooked. What was going to be hard to find out was how he did it and how to make him confess. Albert and Em were dead. He felt a surge of fury. Murdered. They'd been murdered.

He'd dissuaded Stephanie from calling the sheriff. Sam Hodges was bright, but Hank feared he wasn't honest. Sam had been known to go with Peebles on his trips to gambling casinos. No, it would be better to leave the law out of it until they had more evidence than a few saw marks.

The cat had also pointed out the glove. Hank walked into his study and retrieved the glove from the top of the desk where he'd placed it. He turned on the bright light and began to examine the work-stained leather. A small brown stain moved from the thumb up the leather of the glove, ending at the wrist.

Could it be blood?

He got a plastic bag from the kitchen and put the glove in it. It might be a sensible move to have the glove examined by a lab, but first he had to see what he could find out. If there was blood, and it wasn't Albert's, then perhaps they'd be able to match it to the killer.

With the glove safely in a locked desk drawer, Hank found he was pacing the ranch house. He walked from his study down the hall, into the den, around the dining room into the kitchen, circled the kitchen table and repeated the pattern in reverse.

Even though he'd worked a twelve-hour day, he wasn't tired. He wasn't hungry. He finally acknowledged that he wanted to be with Stephanie. No matter that he'd tried to pull back and protect his heart. He was a day late and a dollar short. She'd captured his heart, and she hadn't even tried.

The kiss haunted him because he wanted more. He wanted a lifetime of those kisses, and he didn't know if Stephanie was the kind of woman who made "'til death do you part" promises. He didn't know if he was that kind of man. He'd worked hard not to put himself in a position to find out. Now, though, he'd been unintentionally snared by a woman from a different world.

He sighed and walked to the telephone. The only remedy for what ailed him was a dose of Stephanie. At least on the phone he wouldn't be tempted to sweep her into his arms and take her to a bedroom, any bedroom.

Just as he was about to dial her number, he heard footsteps on his porch followed by pounding on the door.

Junior, one of his wranglers, hurried in, boots clomping. "It's Little Belle," he said. "She's down in the creek and she's going into labor. We need help."

Hank completed the number to McCammon Ranch. Stephanie was closest to the creek, and she had a small tractor they could use if it became necessary to pull the cow out of the creek. The tractor would have a lot more traction in the wet sand along the creek than a truck would.

"Stephanie, it's Hank." He didn't give her a chance to say anything. "Little Belle is down in the creek. We'll set up some lights. Could you bring Rodney and the Kuboto?"

"I'll find you," Stephanie said and hung up.

Hank replaced the phone. His heart was pounding, and it wasn't just from the adrenaline of Little Belle's difficulty. Stephanie hadn't batted an eye. She was ready for action.

At least they aren't making me ride a horse, though this tractor isn't much better. It sways a lot, and let me just say that suspension system isn't a high priority in a farm work vehicle. But this will give me a chance to watch Rodney at work and some of Hank's hands as well.

I want to do a little sleuthing and see if I can find a matching pair of work gloves to the one I found in the destroyed barn.

As much as I enjoy Rodney, I'm finding it difficult to believe he could live on the property and not take notice of someone systematically weakening the structure of a barn. I realize he told Stephanie he heard something, but he made no effort to check on it. I'm concerned. Now I'll get to watch him as he works with Stephanie. If there's any animosity toward her, maybe I can detect it.

The more I think about these murders, the more I believe the answer is right under our noses. Pecos is a small, small town. Most everyone knows everyone else's business. That gives a lot of opportunities for someone to take advantage of others. Nate Peebles is a snake. There's no doubt of that. But is he the only snake? No snake is worse than the one you clutch to your bosom.

Speaking of snakes, it was mighty convenient that two snakes had been let into the house the first day Stephanie comes home. Very convenient. The only one on the premises was Rodney. If I'd had my thinking cap on I would have insisted that Stephanie call the police and have them fingerprint the screen door and all other pertinent surfaces. I'm just glad we got that trap door in her bedroom shut up. No telling what other types of reptiles they might have shoved into the house.

Stephanie is getting on this tractor. Rodney's following on a horse, and Stephanie had the good sense to call a veterinarian before she left the house. I wish

Peter were here. My house human is a dang good vet, and a man who has learned to pay close attention to me when I try to tell him something. In fact, the entire detective agency is due to him and Eleanor, his wife and my mama. I owe everything I am to them, and a whole lot more.

Enough about the past, I'm here in Texas with a murder to solve and a ranch to save. I see the lights in the distance. Oh, my goodness, there's a cow down in the middle of the creek. Two men are in there with her, holding her head above the water. There's Hank, working behind her because...she's giving birth. I read in a magazine that some women were delivering in bodies of warm water, but I don't think this is a good idea for cows or cats.

Stephanie is off the tractor with a rope. She's wading out into the water to see how she can help. She's down on her knees beside Hank. Man, she is something else.

Because I'm a discerning cat and I have a lot of sympathy for the predicament the cow finds herself in, I'm going to stay up here on the bank and remain ready to lend assistance, if necessary. There are very few old wives' tales true about cats, but the one that notes we dislike water is almost universally true. I've seen a few swimming cats, but they are rare and looked upon with question in the feline world. We're landlubbers with great appetites for sea creatures.

I also need this perch to watch Rodney. He's not in the water, but he's on the bank about twenty feet from me. Now he's wading out to help.

What's that commotion in the water?

Oh, look! Stephanie is almost going under as she pulls something out of the water. Two long legs, a head, and here comes the rest of the calf. Rodney is right there to help her.

It's a girl!

And Little Belle is taking a few deep breaths while the boys keep her from drowning. The baby is weak, and Hank is carrying it to the bank. My goodness, it's a pale yellow calf, like a golden retriever, bite my tongue.

Little Belle is struggling to her feet and going after her baby. I think all is right with the world. Here come Hank and Stephanie. He's got his arm around her shoulders. Hmmm. That's more than a friendly squeeze. The way he's looking at her tells me that he has some serious feelings.

And here's the vet.

STEPHANIE FELT like her jeans were glued to her, but it was okay. The cow and calf were just fine. She saw the vet on the creek bank and led Hank over.

"I called Dr. Smith," she explained. "I was afraid surgery would be required." She turned to the vet. "Sorry to trouble you, doctor. I just didn't know."

He shook her hand and then Hank's. "No problem. I was up at the clinic taking care of a horse. I'm just glad it all worked out. What would possess a cow to give birth in the middle of a creek?"

Hank shook his head. "I have no idea. She's one of my best cows. I raised her on a bottle."

"She looks fine now. Want me to give her a once-over?"

Hank agreed and the vet left with Rodney to check out the cow.

"What are you going to name the baby?" Stephanie asked.

"How about Rubber Ducky."

She laughed. "You can't name a cow that."

"That's where you're wrong. I can name her anything I want. And I'll tell you, she's going to have a good long life here on the ranch. Maybe you can use her in some of your rodeo activities."

Stephanie gave him a hug, feeling his wet shirt against her breasts. It was chilling and exciting. When he wrapped his arms around her, she kissed him long and hard. They didn't stop until they realized the cowboys and the vet were watching them.

When Hank released her, she blushed at the sound of good-natured applause from the men.

"Heck, Hank, you got you a new cow and a girl. That's what I'd call a good night," one wrangler said.

Chapter Eight

Wednesday morning broke hot and bright. Stephanie showered and searched through her suitcase for another pair of jeans. She found high heels, three designer suits, several silk blouses, hose and two pair of shorts. Disgusted, she went to the closet where Aunt Em had kept all of her old clothes. She'd already taken her cowboy boots, but the jeans that were left looked worn and disreputable. She had high hopes that Hank might drop by, and she didn't want to be wearing something that looked like she'd pulled it from salvage. There was also the fact that in the past twelve years, her figure had grown fuller and rounder. She was no longer the thin high school girl with braces.

She turned to the black cat who was watching her. "I think I need to have a shopping spree. I also want to make some copies of the will I found in the wall safe and show them to the judge."

The cat winked once and twitched his tail.

"Do you want to go with me?"

The cat nodded.

"Let's do it." She slipped into a sundress and some sandals and headed out the door. "We'll get some groceries while we're out. All of this cooking has depleted Aunt Em's supplies."

She could see the cat agreed with the plan as she put her boots in the back seat. When they got to town, she made a detour and passed the arena. She wasn't dressed for an inspection of the facility, but as soon as she found some jeans she intended to get it up and running.

To that effect she went to the only department store in the whole town. Within half an hour she had a new wardrobe of jeans, shirts and one little red dress selected especially with Hank in mind. She was aware, too, that the salesclerk was watching her.

"Do I know you?" she asked the woman, who was in her mid-thirties, neatly made up, but with a slightly worn look.

"No, but I think I know who you are."

"I'm Stephanie Chisholm."

The woman nodded. "I'm Wanda, Rodney's girl." She looked down at the carpet. "Your aunt talked about you all the time."

Stephanie looked down at the shirt she was holding.

"Your aunt Em was glad you'd made another life than ranching."

Stephanie took her purchases to the counter and put them down. She was surprised at Wanda's revelation. "When was this, Wanda?"

Wanda hesitated. "I saw Em the day before she died.

She was upset about something. Both Em and Albert were terribly upset. They said they wanted out of the ranching business altogether. Like I said, they were upset."

"Do you know what upset them?"

She shook her head. "Rodney noticed it, too. He said he figured when Albert wanted to talk, he would. Rodney wasn't the kind of man to press into other folks' business. Then that storm came through…" She faded to silence.

Stephanie glanced around the floor to make sure no one was within earshot. "Were you out at the ranch a lot?"

Wanda considered. "On the weekends I'd stay some with Rodney." She sighed. "Not too often, though. Rodney had great respect for your aunt and uncle. He didn't want to be carrying on under their noses." She shrugged a shoulder. "Rodney wants to get married."

Stephanie wondered if Wanda wanted to get married, too. There was something about the woman.

"I heard you're selling the ranch." Wanda spoke without emotion.

"No, I'm not."

"But there was a For Sale sign. I saw it."

"There's a lawyer in town who claims to have a new will. As soon as I'm finished here, I'm going over to the courthouse to find the judge in charge of probating wills."

"I wouldn't get in a pissing match with Nate Peebles," Wanda said.

"Why not?" Stephanie knew Pecos was a small town, but it seemed everyone knew her business.

"I hear he's got a mean streak."

"I've got a mean streak, too." Stephanie had the strong feeling that she was being warned off. That Wanda's words were more threat than warning.

"Folks who cross Nate Peebles get hurt."

"Thanks for the information," Stephanie said. She put her sundress back on, paid for her purchases, put them in the rental, and headed to the courthouse. Familiar was nowhere in sight.

If the sun gets any hotter on my black coat, I'm going to have to slink into that local beauty salon and ask for a bleach job. Everything may be bigger in Texas, but it's hotter, too. Why couldn't I have gotten a job in Maine, or Seattle?

Here's a spot of shade in a good location. Actually, a perfection location. I'm well hidden in the shrubs across the street from Nate Peebles's office building. I thought it might be educational to see who visits the lawyer. Chances are it'll just be his normal clients. Maybe I should make a sign—Beware Of Crooked Lawyer. Nah, no one would pay attention. A lawyer friend of Eleanor's told me a joke. What do you call a thousand lawyers in the ocean? A start.

The same could be said of a lot of professions. I'm waiting for the evolutionary moment when the truly superior species, that would be felines, take over the planet. I just hope it's before the ozone layer is depleted and we all fry like eggs on the sidewalk.

Speaking of eggs, I'm a little on the hungry side. This

ranch work gives a kitty a hearty appetite. I'm hoping once Stephanie is done with her shopping spree we can nip into Maizy's and try the breakfast menu.

Okay, there goes a client. No one I recognize from the funeral or around town. Staking out a suspect is one of the more tedious aspects of being a private eye. At least the cops on television get to drink coffee and eat doughnuts. I don't have that option because most people won't take the time to learn to listen to me. So, I'll just swelter here in the heat, my little tummy rumbling, thoughts of salmon with dill churning through my mind. I swear, a fast food burger would be good right about now.

Here comes someone. She's hurrying from the department store where Stephanie was finishing up her shopping. I think it's the clerk who was helping Stephanie. Whatever is on her mind, she's high-stepping it. I wish I could hear through the window, but the glass is too thick and the seal too tight. Maybe I'll mosey around there anyway.

Wait a minute. I recognize that pickup pulling into the parking lot. It's Hank! Why's he going to see Nate Peebles? I'd better hop to the old window, and pronto. I can read lips a bit, and I'll do my best for Stephanie. If nothing else, I can watch the emotion on the faces. That will tell me all I need to know.

HANK WALKED THROUGH the waiting room where a woman in a print dress kept her gaze on the floor. He pushed past the secretary and flung open the door to Peebles's private office. A startled woman looked up, tissue to her eyes.

"I apologize, ma'am, but I need a word with Mr. Peebles alone."

"But I waited half an hour—"

"If you'd like to wait in the café, tell Maizy to put it on Hank's bill." He took her arm and assisted her out of the chair and out the door. He noticed that the woman in the print dress was avidly watching everything. He closed the door.

"Dalton, I'm calling the cops." Peebles lifted the telephone receiver.

"Please do." Hank walked to the desk and towered over him. "Make that call, Peebles. I'd like to tell the cops what I'm going to tell you."

Peebles lowered the phone. "What's eating at you today? If it's the water supply, I can't help you."

"You're the lawyer for Tumbleweed Development?" Hank hadn't known this, but it figured. Where there was a buck to be made, Peebles was there.

Peebles's face changed. "What do you want?"

"The will you managed to cook up for the McCammons isn't going to hold water, Nate. I'd back off it if I were you."

"I have a valid document, signed by both parties."

"What you have is a bad nightmare on your hands. That property was meant to go to Stephanie Chisholm. Her aunt and uncle had made plans for years."

"You have a vested interest in this, don't you?" Peebles was almost sneering.

"My interest is in seeing that Stephanie gets what's hers."

"Your interest is Twisty Creek. What is it? Have you sweet-talked that little lady into giving you water rights?" He laughed. "That's rich. You come in here and accuse me of doing something illegal while you're making time with the McCammon niece to get water."

Hank had the sincere urge to plant his fist into Peebles's face. It was only rigid discipline that restrained him. He clenched his fists at his sides.

"I came to you, man to man. This is how it is—if you try to steal Stephanie's inheritance, you're going to have to deal with me."

Peebles slowly stood up. His face had gone pale, but now it was flushed. "The law is on my side, Dalton. No amount of threats from you can change that. Let me tell you something. I'm going to probate that will Monday, and when I do, McCammon Ranch will be mine. Signed, sealed and delivered. It would behoove you to get your cows off my property. The red Angus are mine. They'll be on a meat truck by Tuesday morning. Every head of them had better be there."

Hank leaned into his face. "Step one foot on that property, Peebles. For any purpose. I'll give you the beating you've deserved for years."

Hank walked out of the office. He was still steaming when he got to the street. It took him a few seconds to see the cat rushing out from the side of the house, but when he realized it was Familiar, he found a smile.

"You are on the scene, aren't you?"

The cat nuzzled around his ankles.

"Where's Stephanie?"

Familiar led the way to the courthouse with Hank striding beside him. Perhaps his visit to Peebles had been rash. He'd gotten up after a night of dreaming about Stephanie. She was such a multifaceted woman. She could do anything she set her mind to. That was both impressive and intimidating. Why would such a woman want the life he had to offer?

His thoughts had been as irritating as his dreams had been sensual. He'd ended up driving to McCammon Ranch only to find that Stephanie had gone into town. When he passed Peebles's office, his action had been spur of the moment. The way he was raised, a man protected a woman. Any woman. But especially the woman who'd begun to creep into his heart. Peebles was trying to hurt Stephanie, so it was the only honorable thing to do—let him know that he'd pay a severe physical price for his harassment.

Still and all, Hank suspected that Stephanie would not be charmed by what he'd done. He only hoped that Familiar would keep his mouth shut. Chances were unless Peebles talked to the police, he wouldn't talk to anyone else.

He felt a snag on his leg. Familiar had hold of him and was looking back the way they'd come. The woman in the print dress was leaving Peebles's office.

"Who is she?" Hank asked. He'd seen her around town, maybe at some dances or barbecues, but he hadn't paid a lot of attention to her. The cat was adamant, though. Something was up with that woman, whoever she was. In such a short time he'd come to rely on Familiar's instincts and tips. He'd scoffed at Stephanie at first, but now he had to concede—there was something dang special about Familiar.

"Should I tail her?" Hank asked.

Familiar's answer was to set out hard on the trail of the woman. Hank followed behind, increasing his stride to keep up with the feline.

"I guess we'll find Stephanie later," he said, glancing back at the courthouse. The woman in the print dress was disappearing around a corner. Hank increased his stride and hurried after the cat and the woman.

STEPHANIE CLUTCHED A COPY of the will in her hand as she came out of the courthouse. The original was in her bra, tucked firmly in the elastic band. The will was her only chance of prevailing. She'd seen a lot of business deals go sour because no one had taken the time to draw up the proper business agreements. The only thing a judge could rule on was documented on paper. If the judge even took her contesting of the will into consideration.

Judge Thomas Bailey had set her teeth on edge. He stated clearly and unequivocally that she had little legal standing. The will Nate Peebles had presented superceded her will. None of her arguments had carried any weight. The judge wouldn't even keep a copy of her will and hardly even glanced at it when she'd asked him to look it over. She had the distinct feeling that Nate Peebles and the judge were close friends.

The one interesting thing had been the judge's reaction when she'd presented her version of the will. He'd been surprised, as if he hadn't expected anyone to contest the will Peebles had produced.

The bitter taste of injustice made her want to wash out her mouth. As she left the courthouse she decided the smartest thing to do would be to rent a safe-deposit box at a bank and put the original copy of her will in a safe place. As she started down the steps she caught sight of Hank and the cat disappearing around the corner of a building. They were moving as if they were in hot pursuit of something.

Silently cursing the high-heeled sandals she'd chosen to wear, she took off after them. After fifty yards, she stopped long enough to remove the sandals and took off in barefoot pursuit.

She caught up enough to see them headed back toward Winchester's Department Store where she'd done her shopping. That was strange. The cat had stayed with her only a few minutes before he'd taken off on his own. Why would he be going there now? She notched up her speed a bit, starting to gain on them, when they turned another corner.

She put on a burst of speed, surprised that it felt so good to run. In the city, the only place it was appropriate to run was the track at her gym or in the park for a jog. Certainly a woman didn't run in a dress while holding a pair of heels in her hand. No, this was strictly a noncity thing to do. She was smiling when she turned the corner. She only had time to see Hank, crumpled on the sidewalk, a pool of blood around his head, before she felt something strike her on the head, hard.

She felt herself falling. She knew the sidewalk would bruise and scrape her knees, but there was no help for it. She was going down and she couldn't stop herself. She tried to turn, to see who had struck her, but her body was beyond her control and blackness was closing down on her fast.

She felt something snatched from her grip and realized that someone had pulled the copy of the will from her hand. She tried to hang on to it, but her fingers wouldn't obey her commands. Before she hit the pavement, she'd fallen into total blackness.

Chapter Nine

Hank felt the grit of the sidewalk against his cheek. Something rough moved across his eyelid. Something rough and annoying. He reached a hand out and felt soft fur. That motivated him to open one eye. Familiar's golden gaze stared into his. In the distance was the sound of traffic, and behind the cat he could see a brick wall.

Slowly the memory came back to him. He'd rounded the corner in pursuit of the woman in the print dress, and someone had bushwhacked him. He sat up slowly and put a hand to the knot on his forehead. His fingers came away covered in blood. It took him a moment to register that Stephanie was lying on the sidewalk beside him, totally still. She was on her side, her knees scraped and bloody and her face pale.

"Police! Help! Police!" Someone screamed behind him.

He ignored the woman's shrill cries as he dragged himself to his knees and felt Stephanie's carotid artery.

Her pulse was strong, and he could see a knot already beginning to swell on her forehead. She'd been struck, too.

What in the hell had happened? He glanced around at the gathering crowd of gawkers, but he didn't see anyone who looked even vaguely threatening. A clerk from a bakery handed him a cold, wet towel, and he used it to bathe Stephanie's face. Her eyelids fluttered, and he leaned over her to block the sun from her eyes.

"Yowey," she said as she blinked several times. "I feel like I rammed my head into a cement wall. My head is aching so bad I think I would feel better if it fell off."

"Someone hit you with something very hard," Hank said. "They hit me, too. Just as I turned the corner."

"Stand back! Folks, move along." A police officer was pushing his way through the crowd. He took in the scene before he walked over. "You folks need an ambulance?"

Hank slowly stood up, ignoring the dizziness that swept over him for a split second. He held Stephanie's hand and helped her up, too, steadying her until she'd regained her balance.

"Officer, I think we're fine," she said.

"What happened here?"

"We were, uh, rushing around the corner and we ran into each other." Stephanie looked right into his eyes as she lied.

Her answer brought a round of twitters from the folks who'd gathered.

"We're okay. I just hope this kind man doesn't sue me," she added.

She was playing it to the hilt, Hank thought, wondering at her strange performance. Why was she trying to protect their attacker? She obviously had her reasons, so he decided to play along with her. "No, ma'am. I'm as much at fault as you are. I wasn't watching where I was going."

"I have to say I've never worked a pedestrian wreck," the officer said, drawing another laugh from the crowd that had begun to disperse.

"Thank you, Officer," Stephanie said. "We'll be fine." She stood beside Hank, waiting for everyone to leave. When they were gone, she leaned a hand against the wall of the building. "I feel a little queasy."

"Could be a concussion. Maybe we should go to the emergency room."

She shook her head. "I'll be fine. I just need a minute. Whoever hit me knocked me out cold."

"Same here."

"Where were you and Familiar going?" Stephanie asked.

"There was a woman in Peebles's law office. Familiar was very interested in her, so we decided to tail her."

"A woman?"

"In a print dress. Familiar was insistent."

"Meow!" Familiar held out one paw with something on it.

The cat's cry drew their attention. Stephanie unsteadily knelt down to see what Familiar had in his claw. It was a little tatter of material.

"That's the dress. Familiar must have jumped on her and snagged a bit of her dress."

Stephanie held the material. She examined it for several seconds before she finally spoke. "That's the same dress Wanda was wearing. Wanda is Rodney's fiancée."

Hank felt another piece of the puzzle click into place even though the big picture wasn't yet clear. "No wonder she didn't want us following her. She was also in Nate Peebles's office."

"But she pointed the finger at Peebles when I talked with her," Stephanie said. "She told me Peebles wasn't anyone to get in a tussle with. Why would she do that?"

"Why would she attack us for following her?" Hank asked. "We have a whole lot more questions than answers."

Stephanie bent down to retrieve the sandals she'd dropped. "Oh, no. The will is gone."

"You had the will with you?" He had a real clear understanding of what had motivated the attack now.

"I had it in my hand with my shoes and now it's gone."

"Damn," Hank said. "Without the will—"

He didn't get a chance to finish. Stephanie reached into the front of her dress and pulled out a document. "That was only a copy. I'm taking the original to the bank right now."

Hank felt a swell of pride. Stephanie was nobody's fool. "Great idea. And I'll lead the way around corners, just in case."

STEPHANIE USED THE BANK bathroom to wash her face and change into jeans and boots. She had the key to her new safe-deposit box in her jeans pocket, and Hank and

Familiar were waiting at the old arena for her. Hank had insisted that he'd rather clean up there than in a public building. Though they both had big lumps and bruises, they were okay.

The attack had only served to give her a whole barrel full of new determination. She was staying on McCammon Ranch, and she was going to turn it into the kind of living trust her aunt and uncle had dreamed about. No one was going to stop her.

She'd convinced Hank not to confront Wanda about what she'd done. It was better if Wanda wasn't aware that they were on to her. That was why, Stephanie had explained, she hadn't wanted to bring the cops into the attack.

Hank had agreed with her reasoning about calling in the law, and he told her what his mother had warned him about. That, coupled with Judge Bailey's reaction to her contesting the will, had forewarned her that local officials weren't inclined to take the side of someone they considered an outsider.

She drove down the street and turned into the arena parking lot. Hank's truck was there. She got out with a sense of anticipation. Everything about her life had changed overnight. The hardest thing she'd ever done was to leave Texas and her aunt and uncle. Now she was back, and she was interested in a man who made his living ranching. Beneath the thrill of excitement she felt at the prospect of seeing Hank, there was also a smattering of dread.

She'd resolved her issues with ranching because

she'd figured a way around the things that bothered her. Hank didn't have the same feelings. When it came time to sell his cattle, he would have no choice but to "head 'em up and move 'em out."

Unless…

She was smiling as she walked into the arena where Hank was inspecting the chutes for the bucking broncs and the bulls.

"How many bulls do you have?"

He looked up. "Bulls? As in male cows?"

She laughed. "That's some kind of lingo for a rancher. Male cows. I'll have to tell your hands about that one."

He came over to her, his desire clear in his green eyes. "Why are you asking about bulls?"

For a moment she thought about forgetting his question and simply kissing him. She shook it off. "I was thinking we should get the rodeo off to a start this Friday night."

His eyebrows moved up in an arch. "Friday night. That would be two days from today."

"Friday night. I could put an announcement in the weekly paper today. I'll bet they'd give it front-page play."

"Are you insane? We can't have a rodeo. We don't have any…" He waved his hands around. "Anything. We don't have anything we need for a rodeo."

"How many bulls?" She was about to laugh.

"Three. And you have three also."

"Six bulls. What about bucking horses? How many?"

He thought a moment. "I don't have any horses that will buck."

She whipped a card from her pocket. "It just so happens that I know someone who can come in and train horses and bulls to buck. I did her advertising for her when I worked in the city."

"*Train* them to buck?"

"Exactly."

"Even if someone can train a horse to buck, can she do it in two days?"

"That's what I'm going to find out." Stephanie retrieved her cell phone from her purse and made the call. They chatted for a few moments and she hung up and turned to Hank. Familiar was watching with great interest.

"Sonja will arrive tonight. She said if we could pick the animals with the most promise, she would teach them."

"Exactly how will we know when an animal has promise?" he asked, looking doubtful.

"You're going to try riding them and we'll see."

HANK HAD GRAVE reservations about what was about to happen, but he grabbed the rope that had been attached around the bull. All he could smell was the sweat of the animal and the dust of the arena floor. He gave Rodney the nod. The wrangler opened the chute, and Hank felt the bull gathering himself between his legs. In one big leap, the bull was in the arena, head down and back legs kicking high in the air. Hank forced his body back and prayed.

When three seconds later he hit the ground, he was

glad he'd gotten bucked clear. Bigboy Mullins, his black Angus bull, had more get-up-and-go than he'd ever imagined. He spit out the dust he'd swallowed, got up and then dove out of the way as the bull bucked by him.

"That's four good bulls," Stephanie said as she marked off the list on her clipboard. She stood beside him, immaculate in a blue chambray shirt embroidered with Texas bluebonnets. She was a vision in her tight jeans, scruffed boots and a straw cowboy hat perched on top of her dark curls.

"What about the horses?" he asked, dusting his jeans. For all that he'd been slung, stomped, kicked, bucked, twisted and finally flung loose, he felt pretty good. It had been too long since he'd tried his luck on a bull.

"Rodney says that two of your hired hands tried out seven. I think with the short amount of time we've had to organize this, that's more than enough. Our biggest entries will come from the barrel racing. And Hank, I've decided that this is going to be an Old West skills rodeo, so we're going to include team penning. I've got one of your wranglers painting numbers on some collars for the cows."

He was amazed at Stephanie's ability to organize. In a matter of hours, she'd gotten stock moved to the arena, animals tested for the competition, a pattern established for the barrels and numbers for the team penning cattle. "Some folks might think team penning doesn't belong in a rodeo," he warned her.

She shrugged. "It's one of the fastest growing sports in the horse world. We have the cattle for it. We'd be foolish not to include it because it isn't a traditional element of rodeo."

"What about a judge?" he asked.

"Good point. I'll find one."

"What about yourself?"

She shook her head. "I think I want to compete in the barrels. Mirage used to be fabulous at it. Of course, we haven't run in years, but most of the other competitors will be out of practice, too. I'm going to have some special instruction for those who've never done it. Sort of a practice session."

"Great idea." It was like Stephanie not to leave anyone out. She wanted everyone to take part and enjoy. "If we could get a mechanized calf, I could do some roping instruction."

She wrote something on her clipboard. "I'll make a few calls." He saw the smile slip off her face. "Do you think people will really buy into this?"

Doubt wasn't her normal emotion, and it made him realize how much she'd bought into the dream. "I do. You know, 'build it and they will come.'"

Her smile returned and he felt as if he'd just delivered the wittiest line in history. Dang. He was acting like a fool, and he knew it. Still, he couldn't help it. Stephanie just did that to him.

They were about to go over the schedule of events when a bright red pickup pulled into the parking lot. Jackie Benton got out and walked over.

"I heard you bought the arena," she said to Stephanie, her gaze drifting back to the pen where the bulls were milling around. "What's going on?"

"Friday night rodeo," Stephanie said. "How about signing up for the barrels or team penning?"

"Maybe a little calf roping on a mechanical calf?" Hank added.

"Good Lord almighty," Jackie said, surprised. "I haven't done that kind of riding in five years."

"Now's the time to get back into it," Stephanie said.

"Okay, sign me up for two teams on the penning and a barrel ride." She was smiling. "This will motivate me to get my flabby self back into shape." She gave Hank a long look. "No roping, though. I'd like to survive this adventure."

Stephanie smiled. "I'm going to do a little barrel practice this afternoon."

"You seem mighty set on staying here in Pecos," Jackie said, squinting against the glare of the sun. "I'm surprised. I'll bet your aunt and uncle would be pleased if they could see it."

"Yeah," Stephanie said. "I'm going to stay on the ranch."

"Has the will thing been settled?" Jackie asked.

Hank stepped forward and put his arm around Stephanie. The one thing he wanted everyone in town to know was that Stephanie wasn't alone. If someone tried to hurt her again, they'd have to go through him. Jackie, who belonged to garden clubs and culture groups, was a great person to spread the news. "As far as we're concerned it has. Stephanie's in residence, and she intends to stay there."

Jackie nodded. "That's the spirit." She gave Hank a curious glance. "It's a good thing she has someone championing her cause, too."

"I couldn't have done all this without Hank."

When she looked at him, Hank felt as if he'd won a prize buckle. She acted like she meant every word of it.

"I know Johnny will be excited. In fact, put him down for the team penning. I'll find us a third. You going to use your uncle's cows?"

Stephanie nodded. "All untrained and untried. It'll be an adventure." She laughed.

"I'll talk to Maizy about providing refreshments, if you'd like. She used to do it before the arena closed."

Stephanie beamed. "That would be great, Jackie. Thanks."

"Whatever we can do to help." She got in her truck and drove away.

Stephanie finished planning the schedule with Hank, and they rode out to McCammon Ranch and then the Running Z to scout the herd for team-penning prospects. The cattle had to be young, and they needed at least thirty head. Hank knew they had plenty to choose from. The trick was going to be in separating the young ones from the herd. It was a good thing they had Biscuit and Banjo to help out. The dogs were excellent at heeling the cows and moving them where he directed.

It had been a long time since Stephanie had really worked cattle, but he watched her closely as she rode into the herd. She moved with her horse as if she'd been doing it all her life. She'd set her eye on one little black heifer, and he watched as Mirage feinted left, then right, and nosed behind the cow to force it away from the herd. It was a pure joy to watch Stephanie ride her mare. If anyone could be born to the saddle, it was Stephanie Chisholm.

As they made their selections, they cut the yearlings out of the herd and pushed them into a corral. It was hard, exciting work. Most of the yearlings were cooperative, but a few tried to break free and run. Those were the ones that required a fast horse with cow sense, and Hank was pleased to see Mirage demonstrate that she'd forgotten none of her training. It was like a game between the cow and the horse, and if a yearling broke bad, he sent one of the dogs after it.

The sun was just beginning to set by the time they had the cattle penned and ready for transport to the arena.

"How about I take you into town and buy you dinner?" Hank asked as he closed the corral gate.

"Are you asking me on a date?" she asked, wiping sweat from her forehead with her bare arm.

"Yes, ma'am, I am." He found he was smiling.

"I accept." She lifted her chin, her hazel eyes sparkling with delight. "On one condition."

"What might that be?"

"No talk about cows or horses or anything regarding the ranch."

He thought about it. What else was there to talk

about? He'd just listen to her then. "You're on. I'll pick you up at eight."

"How should I dress?"

"You were a sight in that sundress this morning."

"That was before I scraped my knees on the sidewalk," she said. "But I'll think of something."

"See you later." She took the reins of the horse he'd borrowed and turned Mirage back to McCammon Ranch. Banjo was at her heels.

Hank watched until she'd disappeared into the horizon. If he wasn't careful, he was afraid he was going to fall so deeply in love that he'd be lost.

Chapter Ten

Stephanie had just slipped into a pair of black, silk capri pants, some sexy, three-strap, high-heels and a black camisole sweater with silver spangles. It was dressy yet casual, perfect for an evening with Hank.

She heard something in the living room and she went to find Familiar sitting in the front window, meowing.

"I'm going out tonight, and I want you to stay inside," she told him. "I want you to be safe, Familiar."

"Me-ow!" His voice was strident.

"You're a determined fellow, I'll say that." She turned away and went back to the bedroom to put on some makeup. Just a touch of smudged liner, a little mascara and some lipstick. She'd just finished when there was a knock on the door. Her heart did a funny little rapid beat as she hurried down the hall.

Hank is early, she thought as she opened the front door. Instead of Hank, Rodney stood there, hat in hand and all cleaned up. "I'm going in to town for a date," he said. "Will you be okay alone?"

She started to tell him that she had a date, too, but she didn't. Wanda and whoever she was working with didn't need to know her business. Besides, she hadn't figured out if Rodney was involved or just unaware. "That's fine."

"You look mighty nice. Are you going out?"

"I'm not certain if I'm going to town or staying here with a friend," she said, forcing a smile. "But you have a good time."

"Will do. My fiancée is a good cook." He smiled. "I'm a lucky man to get her."

"Yes, indeed," she said, gradually closing the door. "Have fun, Rodney."

Before she could shut the door completely, Familiar darted out into the night. She made a grab for him, but he disappeared into a hedge. Hands on her hips, she stood on the porch and peered into the night. She was totally exasperated. The cat knew she would worry about him if he was out in the night alone. "You'd better get in here, you rascal, or I'm going to turn you into stew."

There was a low chuckle and she felt two strong arms wrap around her. "You don't have to threaten me. I'll be glad to step inside with you."

She turned in his arms and lifted her lips for the kiss she'd been thinking about all evening. Hank obliged her, taking his time and making it last. For several moments, she forgot about Familiar, the ranch, everything. Hank was the best kisser she'd ever met. In fact, she could spend days just kissing him—along with a few other things.

When he finally stopped, she sighed. "I have to say, Hank, I enjoy your kisses."

"The feeling is mutual." He stepped away from her so he could take in her outfit. "You look fabulous."

"Thanks." She noted his black jeans and black and red-striped shirt with a string bolo and a black hat. "I return the compliment." Hank was a handsome man who wore his clothes well. Tight jeans were the perfect attire.

"Do you want to get Familiar before we go?" he asked.

"I don't want to leave him out."

He nodded his understanding. "Why don't you get your purse and I'll try to find him. It looked like he went to the horse barn."

"Rodney has gone to town," Stephanie said. "I'll be ready when you come back."

She watched from the porch until Hank faded into the darkness. She was about to step inside when she heard Banjo bark and then begin to growl. She'd never heard the dog sound so vicious. Before she could even react, she heard the dog begin to cry out, as if in pain.

Her impulse was to rush into the darkness and see what was hurting Banjo. Hank was out there, too. And Familiar. All of them were unarmed. If someone had come to the ranch to hurt her or the creatures she cared about, she needed a weapon.

She rushed back in the house and reached into the gun cabinet in the living room and got her uncle's .22 rifle. It was a weapon she'd used before for target practice, and though it didn't have a large bullet, she was deadly accurate with it.

The desperate cries of the dog grew louder as she ran toward the barn. Another sound was mixed in with the dog's yelps. Hank was scuffling with someone. To her horror, there was the sound of a gun discharging.

Hank didn't have a gun and Rodney was gone.

She put on a burst of speed and rushed toward the barn. Halfway there, she heard the sound of a furious cat. It was almost unearthly. It had to be Familiar. Stephanie increased her pace, the gun clutched in her hand.

She heard something like a scream and the sound of a body banging into wood, but she couldn't tell what was happening. It took another ten seconds to get to the barn. At the door she slowed her pace and listened. The horses whirled in their stalls. Banjo moaned softly. Though she listened for footsteps, she couldn't hear anything else.

She stepped into the barn.

It was totally dark, and the sound of her own breathing was loud in her ears.

"Hank!"

There was no answer.

"Banjo!"

The dog whimpered in the darkness.

Stephanie moved along the stall doors. The horses spun and banged against the wood. Stephanie knew where the light switch was, but if she turned it on, she'd be a target as well as the intruder.

"Hank!" She whispered his name, and when there was no response, she felt panic rise in her. She had to stay calm. She had to keep her head. Hank was depending on her. If she lost it now, she wouldn't be able to help him or Banjo.

Her right foot bumped into something and she knelt and felt the dog's thick fur. Banjo whimpered pitifully. She stroked his head and then stepped over him. In the dark she couldn't tell how badly he was hurt. She was steadily making her way to the light switch, listening intently for the sound of someone else in the barn.

Instead in the distance she heard the sound of a vehicle starting. She rushed down the aisle, regretting her choice of heels, and out of the barn by the north exit. She could see headlights across the pasture. Whoever it was had come in from one of the old farm trails across the pasture.

She raised the rifle, her finger squeezing the trigger, but she didn't fire. She couldn't be certain if anyone was between her and the car. If Hank was out there. Her heart clutched painfully at the thought of his potential injuries. The car wheeled and roared across the pasture.

Stephanie could only hope the intruder was gone as she ran back inside and flipped on the light. Hank was propped against a stall door on the opposite side of the barn. His eyes were closed, and she couldn't tell if he was breathing. Blood seeped onto the ground beside him.

Dropping the gun, she ran to his side and knelt, feeling his breath on her hand as she turned his face. He was alive, but she had to find out where he was hurt. The wound appeared to be in his side. His face was also bruised and scraped, and beside him she saw several hay bales and pieces of wood.

She went to the hose and got water and a clean washcloth from the tack room. Kneeling beside Hank, she washed his face. The cold water brought him around.

"Did you get him?" he asked, trying to get to his feet and looking around.

"No, he got away," she said, easing him back into a sitting position. "You've been shot, I think." She fumbled at his shirt buttons, her fingers shaking as she pulled open his shirt to reveal his rib cage covered in blood. The wound wasn't deep, just a crease where the bullet had grazed his skin. She felt an overwhelming sense of relief.

Hank eased to his feet and bent to examine the wound. "The bullet just grazed me. It was the fall from the loft that knocked me out."

"Hank, you could have been killed."

He put his arm around her. "Nothing some antibiotic ointment and a bandage won't cure. How's Banjo?"

They knelt beside the injured dog, who was breathing but wasn't moving. She could see why instantly. His back leg dangled at an odd angle. "Easy, Banjo, we'll get you some help," she said. Kneeling beside him, she stroked his leg while Hank found towels in the tack room.

"We have to get him to the vet," Hank said as he made a sling to carry the dog with as little pain as possible.

"I know," Stephanie said, "but I'm worried about Familiar. He was here. It sounded like he jumped the guy who was after you. Now there's not a sign of him."

"He was up in the loft. He followed me up there after Banjo was hurt." Hank frowned. "I came in and the horses were going nuts. I stopped to pet one when I heard Banjo begin to bark and then cry out. Something moved in the loft, so I climbed up there. Then I saw someone, or thought I did, at the end of the barn. Before I could do anything about it, someone shot at me." He frowned. "It's hard to say, but I think there were two people up in the loft. Familiar got one of them."

"We'll figure it out later. First we have to get Banjo taken care of."

"Why don't you take Banjo to Dr. Smith on Highway 613, and I'll hunt for Familiar."

It was a generous offer, but one Stephanie didn't like. "I think you've forgotten you've been shot. I'll take you to the hospital and then the dog to the vet."

Hank shook his head. "It's just a flesh wound. Really."

"No way," Stephanie said. "You're going to the hospital."

Hank picked up his hat from the barn floor, dusted it against his leg and set it on his head. "If I went to the hospital with this injury, I'd be laughed out of Texas."

"What about infection?"

"I'll let you clean the wound good. It'll be fine. I'm more worried about Banjo."

She sighed. One thing for certain, a Texas cowboy was the most stubborn breed of man on the face of the earth. Arguing with Hank would be like spitting into the wind. "Okay," she said. "But I get to clean it properly."

"Banjo first. Then Familiar. Then the wound." His expression was firm.

"Okay," she said. "It's your wound. I'll take Banjo to the vet and you look for Familiar." She bent down and retrieved the rifle. "There's something with more firepower in the house."

He took the gun, checked to be sure it was loaded and then nodded. "This will do fine. If there's anyone still on the property, I don't want to blow him up, I just want to wing him so I can ask him some questions."

Stephanie looked around the barn. The horses were calming down, but something wasn't right. She stood still for a moment and heard the sound of a low, feline growl. Familiar glared down at her from the hay loft.

She moved toward the ladder that led to the loft. "Hank, I'm going up to check it out." Stephanie put her hand on the ladder, but Hank covered her hand with his.

"Let me."

"I've been in that loft a million times." She kissed his hand and moved hers out from under it and up a rung. "I'm going into the loft. You keep the rifle down here."

"Don't touch anything."

She nodded, then hurried up the twelve rungs of the ladder and into the loft. Halfway up she caught the scent of gasoline. Terror and fury swept over her. She saw the can of gasoline as soon as she cleared the loft floor. Familiar stood beside it, and next to him were matchsticks scattered everywhere. Familiar's left ear was torn and blood dripped slowly into the hay.

"Hank, we'd better call the sheriff this time," she

said, her voice filled with reluctance. "Someone intended to burn the barn down with the horses in it."

"I have a better idea," Hank said. "Let's call a private lab and see if we can get some fingerprints. I've been thinking about what you said earlier. Nate Peebles is in tight with every politician in town, probably even the sheriff. I'm afraid our evidence might get lost."

Stephanie came down the ladder. "Good point. I'm sure we can find some place in Austin to do the lab work."

"When I find out who's behind all of this, someone is going to be very sorry," Hank promised. "Now let's get Banjo to the vet."

"Familiar, too," Stephanie said. "First I'm going to let the horses out into the pasture. I don't like the idea of leaving them in here with that gasoline-soaked hay."

"Good idea." Hank started to pick up a halter, but Stephanie jumped down from the ladder and took it from his hand.

"You're going to rest. That's an order." She put the halter on Flicker and led her from the barn. She came back and haltered Mirage and led her out. It took ten minutes to move all the horses, but when it was done, she gathered Familiar in her arms and Hank lifted Banjo.

"I can't believe Rodney would conspire to burn his horses to death," she said as they walked toward her rental SUV. She opened the back so Hank could gently deposit Banjo.

"I agree. Rodney loves those horses."

"So what are you thinking?" she asked as she opened the passenger door.

Hank got in. "I want to think before I make an accusation."

She nodded, closed the door and walked around to get behind the wheel. "Spoken like a true cowboy. No accusations without the evidence to back it up."

"Once I know for certain…" Hank didn't have to finish. She could see the set of his jaw in the dim interior light of the vehicle.

"THE DOG IS GOOD TO GO. Just be sure you keep the cast clean and dry," Dr. Smith said as he rubbed Banjo's head. "Now for the cat." He picked up Familiar and looked at his torn ear. "This looks like a bite. What kind of animal?" He glanced at Hank.

Hank didn't say anything. He'd known Doc Smith way too long to lie to him about something.

"Possibly human," Stephanie said. "Familiar was defending us."

The veterinarian bent to his examination, and Hank knew he was questioning Stephanie's sanity. Doc gave animals a lot of credit, but a watch-cat was stretching a point.

"There's blood on the cat's front paws, but I don't believe it's his blood," Doc said. Before he could remove his hand, Familiar bit the plastic glove he wore and held on. Doc tried to pull his hand away, but the cat held on.

"What's the problem?" Doc said.

Hank watched the cat. He'd come to greatly respect Familiar's good sense. "Wait a minute. He's trying to tell us something." He saw the look of disbelief on the veterinarian's face. "Don't underestimate the cat."

"What could it be?" Stephanie asked.

Familiar tugged harder on the glove and growled.

"Could it be he doesn't want to be examined?" Doc asked.

"No, it's the glove," Hank said. He remembered the glove Familiar had found in the destroyed barn. There had been a trace of what could be a bloodstain on it. "He's telling us about the glove."

"Hank, has the knock you took on your head clabbered your brain?" Doc asked him.

"Doc, can you remove some of the blood from Familiar's paws? Enough to do a DNA test?"

"A what?"

"DNA. I have a glove with bloodstains on it. If the blood on Familiar's paw matches the blood on the glove, we have a connection."

Doc considered it. "I can prepare the samples for you and send them off to a lab. I can't do the tests here. I don't have the proper equipment." He stroked the cat's head. "But to answer your question, I can get a sample."

"Thanks, Doc."

Familiar held out his paw. "Meow."

Doc took the sample and cleaned up the blood, then nodded at the bloodstain on Hank's shirt. "I see the dog and cat weren't the only ones injured."

"He won't go to the doctor," Stephanie said, rolling her eyes.

Leo Smith motioned for Hank to lift his shirt. "The cat and dog were well behaved for their medical treatment. Are we going to have to restrain you, Hank?"

"I'm fine," Hank said, wishing he could avoid the attention of the old vet and Stephanie. "The bullet grazed me." He felt the cat's golden eyes assessing him. It was almost as if the cat dared him to try to avoid treatment.

"Bullet?" Doc Smith's eyebrows lifted and he frowned. "What in the hell happened out there?"

"Nothing you need to get involved in," Hank said. "The less you know, Doc, the better off you'll be." He started to tuck in his shirt. "If you'll help us get those samples to a lab, that would be plenty of help."

"Take the shirt off. Now," Doc said.

Hank reluctantly unbuttoned his shirt and revealed his ribs. "The wound is more painful than dangerous. It's going to be one of those situations where it hurts most when I laugh."

"No stitches required," Doc said. He went to the counter and came back with a bottle and some cotton pads. "This may sting a little." He patted the cotton pad on the wound.

Hank barely suppressed a groan. Whatever Doc was putting on him was like liquid fire.

"Got to clean it out good," Doc said. "Course if you weren't so stubborn and would go to the emergency room, they might deaden it a little for you."

Hank could see the grin that Stephanie fought. It hovered right at the corners of her mouth. She and Doc had double-teamed him. "It's just a flesh wound," Hank said again, gritting against the sting when the doc applied more of his potion.

"Still hurts, doesn't it?" Doc asked.

"You're a cow doctor and a sadist," Hank managed. "If the cows could sue, you'd probably be in debtor's prison."

"If you had some of the fortitude of a cow and that same ability to keep your lip zipped, I could finish a lot faster."

"Thank goodness I don't need stitches," Hank said. "You'd probably twist a twitch on my lip and ask Stephanie to hold the handle."

"Careful, son, or I might have to stitch those lips together so this young lady here can have some peace and quiet. I've never heard such a racket and a bunch of moaning over a little scrape."

Hank tried not to laugh, but he couldn't help it. Stephanie was looking from one to the other, uncertain what to make of their bantering. "It's okay. He's a pretty good vet for such an ornery cuss."

"I see," Stephanie said. She walked up to the veterinarian. "Will he be okay?"

"He's too mean to kill and too tough to cook. He'll live, if he keeps this clean." He put his tools down. "You'll have better luck with old Banjo there. He's a far smarter patient."

"And Banjo will heal properly?" Stephanie asked.

"The dog will be fine. I don't suppose you want to tell me how he broke that leg, though."

"I wish we knew," Hank said. "Someone was trespassing on the McCammon Ranch. They hurt the dog and the cat and shot at me and then left. You don't need to know that much, Doc."

Doc nodded. "I was afraid there'd be trouble once Miss Chisholm came home. Seems to me Peebles laid claim to the place before Albert and Emily even passed away."

"What do you mean?" Stephanie asked.

"I mean he stopped by here two weeks ago and asked me to go out and vaccinate the cows for Bangs disease. He said they were going to market soon, just as if he knew Albert was going to pass away."

"That's very interesting," Hank said. He put his hand gently on Stephanie's arm, warning her to keep her mouth closed.

"Did he say anything else?" he asked.

"No, just that Albert didn't feel like making the arrangements for the sale, so he'd stepped in to do it. I thought that was peculiar at the time. I just saw Albert and Em together at Maizy's the day before and they seemed fit as a fiddle to me. A big contrast to how Peebles was acting, like Albert was on his last leg."

Hank saw Stephanie open her mouth to speak. He knew he had to stop her. Doc Smith was a good man, but there was no point embroiling him in their mess. "Thanks, Doc. We'll take Banjo and Familiar and be on our way." Hank hesitated. "I'd appreciate it if you didn't say anything about this to anyone."

Doc frowned. "You don't go around poking a snake with a stick. If you suspect someone, you might be smart to tell some folks."

Hank shook his head. "I'd rather not say what I believe right now, but I assure you this is all going to come out sooner rather than later."

"Bring Banjo back in a week. The cat is fine. No need to bring him back." Doc put his hand on Hank's shoulder. "Don't underestimate greed, son. There's a lot of mischief going on in Pecos these days. I hear things." He looked at Stephanie. "You two watch your backs."

It's been a long day and my ear is throbbing, but something is really worrying me. Rodney wouldn't set fire to a barn with his horses in it. But would the firebug have willingly burned up Rodney? Or was it someone who knew he was going into town on a date? I think I want to have a little surveillance on Wanda. I'm torn, though. I feel I should stay at the ranch and protect Stephanie.

Maybe Hank is going to spend the night. That would certainly relieve me of my duties as watch-cat. There are a few things I need. Wanda's last name, an address and some way to let Stephanie know what I'm up to. I don't want her worried about me. She doesn't understand that I can take care of myself, and it's my job to take care of her. Hank is a good stand-in. I think he'd battle the devil to save Stephanie. In a very short time, they've become a team.

That's a good thing, because Stephanie is going to need all the help she can get. I don't know if the local authorities are corrupt are not, but I do know that she can't risk going to them for help. If they are corrupt, they'll know every move she intends to make. She'll be a goner before she even gets a chance to have the proper will read.

What happened in the barn tonight is just one sam-

ple of the danger. The bad guys were willing to burn down a barn with twelve horses in it. That's cold. That's the kind of warning that can't be ignored. There were two people in the loft. I got hold of one of them, but the other got away clean. The good news is that whoever I attacked will show the marks for some time to come. That gives me some measure of relief.

All of this excitement and action has made me ravenous. As soon as we get back to the ranch, I'm going to let Stephanie know I need something to eat. I'm thinking something chilled and delicate. I'm sure Hank will agree.

Chapter Eleven

Stephanie blinked awake just as the sun was lighting her room with pink. Something rough was rasping the skin of her left foot. She pulled her leg up to avoid the tickling sensation and sat up to find Familiar ready to pounce on her other foot.

"What is going on?" she asked.

"Meow." Familiar jumped to the windowsill and batted at the closed window.

He wanted out, and no doubt about it. She got up and opened the window. She watched the cat leap to the ground and tear off toward the barn. She didn't need a reminder that gasoline was in the hayloft and had to be dealt with. She pulled a robe on over her lime-striped pajamas and hurried into the living room. Hank was still sound asleep on the sofa.

She stood for a moment watching him as he inhaled and exhaled. She could study him now. He had tiny crinkled lines around his eyes where he'd worked in the sun, and his dark hair was slightly curly. Had he chosen to wear it any longer, it would have been beautiful. There was a tiny scar on his chin, as if he'd fallen as a child and cut it. His eyelashes fanned on his cheek with the length and fullness that any girl would envy. That was offset by the shadow of a heavy beard. He was a man's man, every inch of him.

"I hope you see something you like," he said, opening his eyes.

"I didn't know you were awake," she said, feeling a little guilty. She'd been staring pretty hard.

He sat up and smiled. "Thanks for loaning me the use of your sofa."

She considered what she might reply and decided on the truth. "I hope one day you spend the night and choose to share the bed with me."

Hank stood up slowly. "You're not a woman to beat around the bush, are you?"

She shook her head. Never before in her life had she been so direct with a man. She'd changed since coming to Pecos. She'd changed since meeting Hank. In the past she'd always been afraid of showing her feelings, of caring for someone who might tie her down. Hank was about as tied down as a man could be. He had ten thousand acres and over a thousand cattle. Somehow, though, he didn't strike her as a man who would be an anchor.

"I lost this life once before," she said. "I was so busy running I couldn't see what I was leaving behind. I don't want to lose it again."

"You really want to stay here in Pecos?"

She heard the disbelief in his voice. "I can tell you again and again, but you won't believe my words. I'll just have to show you." She smiled. "I'm not leaving this ranch."

He took a step toward her and gently tipped her chin so that he stared deep into her eyes. "A woman like you could be a lot of heartache."

"How could I be more than any other woman?" she asked.

"Because you're a surprise at every turn. After you, most women would be plain boring."

She stood on tiptoe and kissed his chin. "I'm not sure that's a compliment, but I'll take it as one."

"Oh, believe me, it's a compliment," Hank said.

"We'll talk about this later," Stephanie said, touching her cheek with the flat of her palm, "when it's dark outside and we don't have a million things to do." She kissed him lightly. "How's your wound?"

"Sore and stiff, but once I move around, I'll be fine."

"I'm going to meet Sonja, the trainer, at the arena. What are your plans for today?" She didn't want to take her eyes off him. Even a little stiff, he moved with more grace than anyone she'd ever known.

"How about I meet you up at the arena? I want to get the gasoline out of the hayloft and retrieve the glove and take it to Doc so he can send off the DNA samples."

"Good idea. What about lunch at Maizy's?"

"Noon?" he asked.

"Perfect." She kissed his lips lightly once more, lingering, savoring. She felt her knees weaken at the anticipation of a deeper kiss. Sighing, she stepped away from him. "Familiar has taken off toward the barn. I'm about to give Banjo his antibiotics and some pain medication. He's not feeling great, but his eyes are bright."

"I'm going to talk to Rodney this morning and see what he knows about that gasoline."

Stephanie nodded. "He's going to wonder why all the horses are out."

"Don't worry, I'm going to paint him a vivid picture."

Stephanie didn't doubt it, but she had another thought. "Maybe while you're talking to Rodney, I'll check out his apartment in the barn. There's the chance we might find something that leads us to the intruder."

Hank nodded. "That's a good idea. Then we can go into town together."

"Familiar thinks we're slackards. He's already out there snooping around. You're welcome to the shower in the blue guest bedroom. I'll get cleaned up and dressed and then meet you at the kitchen in ten minutes."

"Then I'll escort you to the barn. We don't want a black cat to outdo us."

Stephanie had just poured two cups of coffee when Hank appeared in the kitchen doorway, his hair still damp from the shower. He took the cup she offered and sipped. "Thanks."

As they walked across the yard to the horse barn, Stephanie caught sight of movement in the hayloft. She nudged Hank and drew his attention to the shadow that moved across the open door.

"Someone's up there," he whispered. "You go

through the door and make sure whoever it is doesn't come down the loft ladder. I'm going to climb that old silo and see if I can't swing over to the loft door."

Stephanie gauged the distance. It was going to take a mighty good swing or Hank would end up dangling twenty feet above the ground. "Be careful," she said softly and touched his chest with her hand.

He took off and she waited until he was at the silo before she walked into the barn. "Rodney!" she called. The wrangler might have already gone to catch the horses. "Rodney!"

The door to his apartment swung open and he stepped out. "Why are the horses out, Miss Stephanie?" he asked.

"There was a problem in the loft. I thought they'd be safer outside."

A frown touched Rodney's face. "What kind of problem?"

"It's a long story." She maneuvered so she was right beside the loft ladder. If someone was up there, he'd have to come down the ladder or jump out the loft door with a twenty-foot fall through open space.

"What's that?" Rodney turned to look up toward the loft.

She heard the cat's growl as clearly as Rodney. "Someone's up in the loft," she said. "Someone who tried to set fire to the barn last night."

He grabbed the ladder. "I'm going up to catch him."

"No! Rodney!" Before she could stop him, he was climbing the ladder. "Rodney, don't!"

She saw the seventy-five pound bale of hay toppling end-over-end down the ladder before Rodney did. He threw up his hands to try to block the bale, but the momentum of the hay knocked him backwards off the ladder. He hit the barn floor with a thud, the hay on top of him.

"Rodney!" Stephanie ran to him and pulled the bale off him. He was breathing but dazed. Before she could do anything a man leapt down the ladder, hit the dirt floor of the barn and ran outside. He was lean and well built with a fast sprint. Other than that, Stephanie didn't see his features. She was too busy with Rodney. If the wrangler was in cahoots with the intruders, they certainly didn't value him since they'd deliberately tried to kill him just to create a diversion.

"Hank, are you okay?" she called up. "Rodney's hurt down here."

"I am okay," Hank said from the edge of the loft. "What happened?"

She told him briefly as he jumped down and went in pursuit of the intruder. Stephanie knelt beside Rodney. The wrangler was coming out of the daze and shaking his head, as if to clear it.

"Who tried to kill me with a hay bale?" he asked.

"He got away," Stephanie said. She looked out the barn door. Hank was coming back, anger in his stride. "Did you see him?" she asked.

He shook his head. "He was too far away. He had a horse tied out."

"A horse?" Rodney eased into a sitting position. "What color?"

"Chestnut," Hank said.

Rodney frowned. "That's a common color."

Hank caught Stephanie's eye, and she understood what he wanted. "Rodney, last night someone was in the hayloft. They had gasoline and matches. If it hadn't of been for Hank, Familiar and Banjo, they would have burned the barn down with the horses in it."

The impact of her words made Rodney even paler. "Who would do such a thing?"

"That's exactly what we intend to find out," Hank said. He put his arm around Stephanie and drew her close. "Someone will go to any lengths to try to run Stephanie off her family's ranch."

Stephanie was glad for the feel of Hank's arm around her shoulders. She felt as if her life had spun dangerously out of control. A week before she'd been putting out fires in advertising campaigns. Now, she was literally in danger of seeing her ranch and her animals deliberately torched. It made her feel helpless and furious.

"I can't think who would do such a thing, Miss Stephanie," Rodney said. "But one thing I guarantee is that I'll help you do everything possible to catch whoever it is."

"We're going to find out who's behind this and put them behind bars for a long time," Hank said. "To that end, I think we should search the hayloft right now. That man came back here during broad daylight because he must have left something important behind. If he didn't get it just now, there's a chance we can find it and identify him."

Stephanie realized both Hank and Rodney were trying to lift her spirits. She looked down when Familiar head-butted her ankle. The cat, too, was trying to lift her spirits.

"Okay, guys," she said. "Together we'll figure this out. Let's get busy."

The bipeds are searching the loft. It's a little late. The man had something clutched in his hand when he left. That must have been what he came back for.

The thing I learned this morning is that Rodney isn't involved. He was sleeping like the proverbial dead when I inched open his apartment door and took a little tour. He's a professional bachelor, and his life on the ranch is pretty darn good. He has free room and board, and all the amenities. He'd be nuts to mess it up, and I honestly thing he's fond of the ranch and Stephanie. If he's involved, it's through that woman he's so in love with.

He had a photo of the notorious Wanda Nell Hempstead. She lives at 3232 Minora Lane, which is on the east side of town. Now that I know where I'm going, I'm sure I can get there. She's in this up to her eyeteeth, and I wouldn't be a bit surprised to find out that she's involved romantically with Nate Peebles. Rodney loves her, but Nate has power and money. Love versus power, and she's made the wrong choice. It's the wrong choice every time, but I see plenty of bipeds make it over and over again. What a shame.

My goal for the rest of the day is to get into town. I believe Stephanie intends to go to the arena, so I'd best

*get myself up to the house and by the SUV before she
leaves me behind. I have some sleuthing to do in the fair
city of Pecos. I might even pay a call on the courthouse
and check out some deeds and property. Mostly, though,
I want a match on the blood from the man I attacked last
night, and again this morning, and the glove that was
found in the collapsed barn.*

*I realize all the evidence points at Nate Peebles, but
somehow, that's just too convenient. Peebles is in it, no
way around it. I don't believe he's the top, though. My
theory is to squeeze him to see who he gives up.*

*I also want to get my paws on that creep who was
going to toast some horses and a dog. Horses are de-
fenseless against something like a fire when they're shut
up in a barn. Canines are not nearly as evolved as felines, but they are still noble creatures. Banjo is the
hardest working dog I've ever seen. He seems to thrive
on chasing cows hither and yon—an activity that seems
hot and dirty to me. I mean really, if the cows wanted
to move somewhere, they'd do it on their on, wouldn't
they? Whether I understand it or not, Banjo does his job
well, and he's had a rough week. That someone could
kick a dog hard enough to break his leg is beyond me.*

*One last thing I hope to accomplish in town is to look
for a man with scratches on his face. Deep scratches. I
got my hooks into the guy good in at least four places.
If he's walking around Pecos, I'll be able to identify him,
and maybe give him a little more of what he deserves.*

Meanwhile, Miss New York City is making goo-goo

eyes at the Lone Ranger in the front yard. I'd best bust 'em up and get 'em to work or we'll never resolve this case.

HANK WIPED THE SWEAT from his forehead and put his straw cowboy hat back on. Cogar, a big gray known for his willful attitude and practical jokes, went by in a perfect sunfish. He hit the ground hard and went straight up again. Kimberly Seick, a young woman who'd arrived with the horse trainer, held on for all she was worth. When the buzzer sounded, Kimberly jumped to the ground, a huge grin on her face. "He's some kind of rodeo horse," she said as she dusted off her hands. "Wow."

If someone had told Hank a woman could train horses to buck in half a day, he would never have believed it. Sonja Kepler had shown him otherwise, and Kimberly, her assistant, had just demonstrated it.

"Horses can be trained for many activities. Especially something that is joyful. Bucking is a natural part of play. Some horses are just more talented at it than others," Sonja said as she sipped an icy cola and leaned against the rail of the arena. "That gray has exceptional talent as a bronc. And one that loves his job, not one that's forced to do it with pinch straps."

"I second that," Kimberly said as she grabbed a cold drink. "I've ridden Dasher, Scrapiron, Nugget, M&M, Gus, Hawk and Cogar. That's the seven. I think all of them can give a good show for you. The best thing is that come Saturday, they'll be ready to move cows or take a trail ride."

Sonja patted the girl's arm. "You'll be taking over my business soon. You have great talent." She turned to Stephanie who'd just finished checking out the new PA system she'd had installed. "What else do you need?"

Stephanie gave her a hug. "For now, maybe just some good thoughts."

"If you'd like, Kimberly and I can stay and give a demonstration on positive, nonabusive training. We could ask for a volunteer horse from the audience, and show everyone how much easier it is to train with kindness instead of brutality," Sonja offered.

"You'd do that?" Stephanie's smile was a million watts.

Hank felt his own mouth turning up. He'd never seen things fall together so well. It was almost as if the rodeo was intended. The broncs and bulls had learned to do their work without any harsh measures. He was pretty well amazed at the three women who stood beside him.

"Please, it would be invaluable to folks around here," Hank said. "A lot of folks aren't taught how to work with their horses except by force. This could open a lot of doors."

"Then we'll stay," Sonja said. "I have to admit, I'm a little curious to see how this is going to work out. A humane rodeo. That's an interesting concept."

Hank basked in the happiness on Stephanie's face. A week before, he never would have believed he'd fall in with such new ideas. Now that he'd seen it, though, he was a believer. Far be it from him to get stuck back in the dark ages when animals were trained with a whip.

He watched as Stephanie picked up her clipboard and

began to go over her notes. They all looked up when a truck and trailer pulled up beside the arena. Jackie got out and went back to the trailer to unload her big paint mare. "I thought I'd give Buttercup a chance to work in an arena before the show tomorrow night."

"Sure," Stephanie said. "Help yourself. We're done for now."

Jackie tacked up her mare and rode over to them. "The word is spreading through town like wildfire. Everyone is talking about you and what you're doing for the town."

"Good," Stephanie said.

Hank could see how pleased Stephanie was. She was going to pull this off and win a lot of support in the process.

"I'm going to post the arena rules," Stephanie said. She pulled a sheet of paper from her clipboard and handed it to Hank.

He read through it quickly. "Who's going to determine 'poor horsemanship'?" he asked.

"Me," she said without batting an eye.

That, he had to concede, was one of the reasons he'd begun to fall in love with her. She was as hardheaded as a Brahma bull and as stubborn as a mule. And she stood up for what she believed in.

They both turned to see Jackie loping around the arena. She made a turn and came back toward them. "I almost forgot. Johnny's out of town tomorrow night. Could I get the two of you to ride with me for the team penning?"

Hank waited to see Stephanie's reaction. He wasn't disappointed when she looked at him and said, "Will you?"

"Sure," he said. "We'll ride a team."

"Johnny's going to be bitterly disappointed," Jackie said. "It was a stroke of brilliance to include team penning in the list of competitions."

"We want to focus on the cowboy arts," Stephanie said. "It's a little different take on the idea of rodeo, but this is a different kind of rodeo."

"We're going to beat the socks off everyone else in town," Jackie said.

"That's the plan," Hank answered with a grin.

STEPHANIE CRUISED down Main Street looking for Familiar. It had occurred to her at lunchtime that the black feline was missing. She wasn't worried, exactly, but she was concerned. The cat had gotten out at the arena with them, and she couldn't remember the last time she'd seen him. In fact, once she left the car, she couldn't remember seeing him at all.

Where could he have gone? He might be able to buy fancy dinners on credit in New York, but it was highly unlikely an unescorted cat would even get his front paw in the diner in Pecos. So, where had he gone?

She turned left, circled the town on a back street and cruised down Main again. Wherever he was, he was well hidden. She'd dropped Hank off at Maizy's so he could talk with her about concessions for the rodeo. Jackie had made the initial contact, but Hank wanted to check the details. When she couldn't find Familiar, she drove down Main Street once more and headed toward the diner to join Hank. She was starving. Her stomach had grown to her backbone she was so hungry. Hungry to see Hank again, too.

She couldn't help thinking about him as she drove through town. He was like a knight on a white horse, riding to her rescue. What in the world would she have done without him? That question didn't bear answering. She did have him. She thought about his chivalric stance about sleeping on the sofa. She'd been disappointed, but she understood.

Stephanie had always lived a cautious romantic life. She wasn't the type of woman to get involved in casual flings, and she'd been surprised at her directness with Hank. She wanted him in a physical way that unsettled her. She was normally better able to control her needs and urges. Hank, though, was like an addiction. She wanted to be with him, to touch him, to listen to him. And she wanted him to hold her and make love to her.

Part of what was so attractive about him was that he wasn't easy to seduce. He had a sense of right and wrong, and that was incredibly appealing. He had no intention of getting involved in any physical way, unless he could follow through with a real relationship. It was refreshing and terribly exciting to know such a man.

It was a good thing kissing wasn't off-limits, because she adored kissing him. She could kiss him all afternoon. In fact, when she got to the restaurant, she might call him into the hallway where the bathrooms were located and kiss him right there.

She might— She slammed on brakes. Familiar had darted out of the department store, close on the heels of Wanda the salesclerk. Stephanie did a U-turn on a back street and sped back to the corner. She took a right, then another, and finally another and ended up at the intersection a block behind them. From her vantage point behind an old Western Auto, she watched Wanda stride down the street, oblivious to the cat following her. Stephanie eased forward, following. Whatever Familiar was up to, she intended to give him backup.

Chapter Twelve

Hank checked his watch. It was nearly one o'clock. Stephanie was at least thirty minutes late, and though he'd borrowed Maizy's phone to call her twice, she hadn't answered her cell phone. He was deeply worried. This wasn't what he expected of Stephanie. He was afraid she'd gotten into some kind of trouble when she went to hunt Familiar.

The cat had a knack for being in the right place at the right time. Like the barn loft. He'd saved Hank's hide, and possibly his life. Had Stephanie followed the cat into some difficulty?

He stood up.

"Something wrong with the iced tea, Hank?" Maizy asked. She was in her early fifties and one of Hank's favorite people in town. For all of her teasing, she was a compassionate person.

"I'm not sure," he said. "If Stephanie Chisholm comes in here, ask her to please wait." He started to leave and turned back. "And tell her to turn her cell phone on."

"Sure thing, Hank." Maizy's smile was lighthearted. "I'll handle your romantic problems and serve you the best lunch in town. Fact is, though, I never figured you'd fall for a city girl."

"Fact is, Maizy, that's for me to worry about," Hank said as he pushed through the door and left. He softened his words with a friendly wave as he left.

Stephanie had taken the vehicle after she'd dropped him off at the café. She'd expected to be gone no more than five minutes while she swooped through the town to look for a sign of Familiar. Where could she be?

He was frustrated that he had no vehicle, and at last he decided he had to call one of his wranglers to bring his truck. He went back inside Maizy's and borrowed her phone again. In less than two minutes, he was outside, waiting for Junior to bring his pickup.

While he waited he walked down Main Street. The town looked as if it had closed for the noon hour. No one stirred in the growing heat of late spring.

He stepped into an inset doorway of an insurance office to get out of the sun. When he glanced to the right, he was surprised to see the woman who'd worn the print dress, Wanda, hurrying toward him. Opening the door of the insurance office quietly, he stepped inside. Wanda rushed past him and entered the local newspaper office next door.

"Can I help you?" a woman asked behind him. He turned to discover that the secretary in the insurance office was staring at him curiously.

"I wanted to check the rates on farm vehicles," he

said. It wasn't an out-and-out lie. He had intended to do this, but right now he needed a place to wait until Wanda left the newspaper office.

"Have a seat," the secretary said. "I'll need a list of your vehicles."

"I'll have to go home and write them all down and come back," Hank said, opening the door. "Thanks." He was gone before she could register a question.

He made sure Wanda was gone from the newspaper office and went inside. "The woman who just left, what did she want?"

The young man at the desk looked over his glasses. "I'm afraid that's none of your business," he said.

Hank knew he had to think fast. "Look, she's my sister and she's been in a lot of trouble lately. I'm just trying to keep her from making more trouble for herself."

"What kind of trouble?" the reporter asked.

"Well," Hank played it to the hilt, looking down at his boots and shaking his head, "she's sort of a chronic liar. She starts stuff, just for the excitement, and then it blows up in her face. She's already being sued in Austin, and the newspaper that printed her story is also named in the suit."

The reporter was young and he looked worried. "The paper was sued?"

"Big money. So whatever she told you, I'd be sure and check it out before you print it."

"She said there was an epidemic of swamp fever at McCammon Ranch," the reporter said, picking up a notebook. "She said eight horses were down with it and that it was highly contagious. She said she was doing the folks in town a favor so they wouldn't catch it at the rodeo."

"Thank goodness I caught her in time," Hank said, not showing the anger he felt. "There's no swamp fever. All the stock at McCammon Ranch is fine, as are the animals involved in the rodeo. I'm glad we cleared this up."

"Me, too," the reporter said. "You can tell your sister if she ever comes in here again, I'm going to call the law."

"I hate to say it, but I agree with you," Hank said. "Thanks." He headed out the door just in time to see Stephanie driving up, Familiar in the front seat.

His heart rate increased about twenty-fold, and he couldn't help the smile that spread across his face at the sight of her. She stopped the SUV and leaned over to throw the door open for him.

"Hop in," she said. "I've got a story to tell you."

STEPHANIE NOTICED the amused look on Maizy's face as she followed Hank into the restaurant. The café proprietress didn't bat an eye when she ordered for the cat.

"He likes the shrimp grilled," Stephanie said.

"Whatever he wants," Maizy said. She tapped Hank on the shoulder with her pad. "What about you?"

"I'll follow Familiar's lead," he said. "The cat is a connoisseur of fine foods and good company."

"I never thought I'd see the day," Maizy said, pouring iced tea for the humans. "Milk for the cat?"

"In a saucer, please," Stephanie answered.

When the waitress was gone, Stephanie glanced

around the café. No one was sitting close enough to overhear her conversation. "I think Familiar found the man who tried to set fire to the barn."

"Where?" Hank asked.

"He was in Coleman's drugstore. He was in the section where the antibiotic salves are. I'd been following Familiar and Wanda. She went in a dime store and Familiar must have seen something that caught his interest, because he took off down the street to the drugstore. By the time I got there, he was waiting outside, so I parked and we walked in. By the time I caught up with Familiar, the man was running out of the drugstore. We followed him, but I lost him at the end of town."

"Did you get a tag number on his vehicle?" Hank asked.

Stephanie shook her head. "We didn't get close enough. But I did go back to the drugstore and tried to identify him. No one remembered seeing him."

"They didn't remember a man with a scratched-up face?" Hank was angry. She could see it in the high color along his cheek bones.

"I don't think he talked to anyone, Hank. The only people there were the pharmacist in the back and a young salesgirl who was reading a magazine. I think she was telling the truth."

"Okay." He sipped his tea. "It's just that we can't seem to get a lead on these people. They attack us, try to burn the barn, hit us on the head with lumber and we can't catch them."

"We will."

Hank told her about Wanda and the story about swamp fever in the horses.

The more he told her, the angrier Stephanie got. "I ought to go over to that department store and snatch her baldheaded," Stephanie said.

He laughed. "Now it sounds like you never left Texas. A hair pulling." He laughed again. "Maybe we could include that as one of the rodeo events."

Stephanie laughed, too. "It's a figure of speech. I didn't mean it literally." Her mouth crooked up on one side. "But it isn't such a bad idea now that I think about it."

"It means you're getting to them. If they're so afraid of the rodeo that they're trying to shut you down before you even get started, that means they're afraid of what you might accomplish."

She nodded. Hank had a way of seeing everything in a light that made her feel better. "Thanks. So what are we going to do?" She realized, as she said the words, that she viewed Hank as her partner. This man she was so physically attracted to was also someone she felt she could count on.

"I think Familiar has the right idea. A little reconnaissance. We need to find out who Wanda is really working for."

"Good idea. What about tonight?"

He nodded. "Perfect."

"I should go home and take a shower," Stephanie said. She was more than a little gritty. Sonja and Kimberly had worked all morning at the arena, and she'd helped them.

"Would you like me to wash your back?" Hank asked.

She studied him. If she took him up on his offer, she would be making a commitment. He wasn't the kind of man who wanted a casual relationship. He'd made that clear enough. "What if things don't work out and I lose the ranch?"

He reached out and stroked Familiar's head. "I've thought about that on and off all morning. I don't think anyone would ever accuse a rancher of playing it safe. It's the most unpredictable business in the world. But in a lot of ways, I have been too cautious. Emotionally cautious."

Stephanie couldn't take her gaze off him. He might have played it safe romantically in the past, but he was confronting it head-on now. Hank was the most honest person she'd ever met. She was in awe of his courage. "I don't think you're alone there, Hank. The idea of falling in love with someone, of becoming so dependent on someone else that if something happened to them…" She could feel the lump building in her throat. "I guess I've lost too much in my life. When my parents divorced, it was the end of my world. Now Uncle Albert and Aunt Em are dead. I've been afraid to love again. What if something happened and I lost that person?"

He took her hand. "What if you decide to leave this life and Texas? What if you aren't happy here? I could lose you as easily in that way as another." He gave her time to think. "Those are the risks we both face, Stephanie."

She swallowed. "You're right." Her eyes were brimming with unshed tears, but now wasn't the time to cry.

She was happy. Terrifyingly happy. In a matter of a week her life had changed in a way she could never have predicted. Some of it was sad and painful, but so much of it was good. This man of honor, a good man with a desire to help her, had walked into her life. "Whatever the risk, I want to take it," she said.

His smile was dazzling. He stood up. "Maizy," he called, "better put those three orders in to-go boxes. We've got something we have to do."

Maizy came out of the kitchen. She took one look at the two of them and her eyes crinkled in a smile. "Well, well, I'll bet I could guess what it is, but maybe I'll just hush."

"Smartest move you've made all day," Hank said, taking Stephanie's arm. "Familiar, you ready?"

The cat hopped to the floor and started toward the door. Hank took the three boxes of food. His truck was sitting outside the café. "I'll meet you there," he said.

Instead of getting in the SUV with Stephanie, Familiar sauntered down the street. When Stephanie called him, he ignored her.

"I think he has business here in town," Hank said, watching the cat.

"We'll come back and get you in a few hours," Stephanie called to him.

Familiar turned around and blinked twice, then he disappeared around the side of a building.

I realize the humanoids feel they've discovered the wonder of love. I suppose it's a good thing. It keeps me young and ever hopeful to see the antics of lovers. But I have a case to solve. I'm glad to be in town alone. The bipeds are too conspicuous for true surveillance. I can slip from shadow to shadow and never be seen.

Speaking of shadows, now would be a good time to find one. Hank's two wranglers, Junior and Patrick, just cruised down Main Street. I assume they're in town to bring Hank's truck. The interesting thing about small towns for an investigator is that most everyone knows everyone else. It's that obvious pattern that often works to conceal. Now I'm just going to saunter over to the courthouse and see what I can dig up. I'm very curious about Wanda Hempstead's marital status. She's a woman of a certain age, which is a kind way of saying she's pushing forty if she's a day. One would think she might have been married by that age. If she's dating Rodney, she should be divorced. But who was she married to? What's her maiden name? There are lots of questions to be asked here, and I'm just the detective to get the answers.

I did a count in the phone book and there are ten lawyers in town. It'll be interesting to see which lawyer handled her case.

The thing I regret about this is the grilled shrimp that are being transported, as we speak, to hacienda Mc-Cammon. I hope Stephanie keeps them chilled. I'm not going to count on it, though. I don't think she's too concerned with food right at this moment. Ah, young love.

Now I'm at the courthouse. It was simple enough to get in here with Stephanie, but I don't think anyone will open the door for me alone. I'll just have to do my best to lurk. Okay, here comes a man in a suit. He's so pre-occupied reading the papers in his hand I don't think he'll notice if I slip in with him.

Perfect! I'm in.

I love these old courthouses where all of the county offices are kept together. The only addition here is the jail, and I hope one day, in the near future, to be able to put a few more people in it.

Here's the clerk's office where the divorce decrees are kept. It's rather hard to be inconspicuous inside the building—all this pale tile. Lucky for me someone has a green thumb and has put two potted plants outside the door. Fancy that. But I can hang out here until some-one opens the door.

There it is. A pretty young girl headed for the ladies' room, I suppose. But I'm inside. It's nice and cool here, and there's the vault. It'll take a bit of work, but I'll find the proper book. Uh, oh, I've been spotted!

I'll give this nice lady a purr and a little sandpaper kiss. Ah, she's eating out of my hand. She's a cat per-son, and she isn't a bit distressed that I'm in the stacks. If I use my charm, I'm sure she'll help me find what I'm looking for. I just have to be able to convey to her what I need.

She's stroking me and looking around. There's a computer back here. That's the ticket. I'll hop over and type. Wanda Nell Hempstead. She's looking at the screen and then at me. She's considering. I think she might be a little frightened of me. It's just a normal case where a biped has never considered the possibility of a cat who can read and write. Just wait until I write my memoirs! Humanoids will have to acknowledge the superior intellect of the feline then.

She's catching on. I can see it in her eyes. She's going to some files and looking something up. Now she's going to a book and pulling it down. She's bringing the book over to the desk and opening it.

Wanda Nell Hempstead vs. Martin Beech. Dang, that doesn't mean a thing to me. Nate Peebles was her lawyer, though. She was granted a divorce on the grounds of incompatibility. It's a short, sweet and to the point document. Drat, I was hoping for more.

No sense crying over spilt milk though. In fact, the woman is walking back in here with a carton of milk and a saucer. She's a very nice woman. Matilda Richey is her name. If I can think of something to do to repay her for all of these kindnesses, I sure will.

Then again, maybe just a little bit of sandpaper tongue, a few purrs and some figure eights around her ankles is enough. She's opening the door for me to escape. Yet again I am delighted by the astute nature of some bipeds. I do think they can be trained.

Chapter Thirteen

Stephanie closed the blinds in her bedroom. She was totally conscious of Hank's gaze on her. He was drinking her in, absorbing every move. She got a silky black robe from her closet and walked up to him and took his hand. She led the way into the bathroom and started the shower. She'd never considered taking a shower with a man in her aunt and uncle's house. Now, though, she was glad they'd build such a spacious bath for her when they'd remodeled her bedroom.

She felt Hank's hands on her shoulders, turning her to face him. The look in his eyes was almost more than she could take—her knees grew weak with longing. She stood on tiptoe and kissed him, putting all of her hopes and desires into the kiss.

She felt his hands caressing her back, slowly moving to the front and beginning to unbutton her blouse. The water was running and the room was filling with steam. It was almost like a dream, one she had no desire to ever awaken from.

She stepped back so she could unbutton his shirt only to discover it was closed with Western snaps. Her lips tugged up into a smile as she popped them open one by one.

"What's so funny?" he asked, lifting her chin with one finger.

"I can't believe I've fallen in love with a cowboy," she said. "I get the funny feeling that somehow Uncle Albert and Aunt Em are directing my life from the other side."

Hank smiled. "If they're on my side, I'll take all the help I can get." He kissed the corner of her mouth. "Whatever it takes to make you smile, that's what I want for the rest of your life."

"You make me smile," she said. "You make me strong and able to do what I need to do."

He kissed her as he peeled her blouse down her arms. His fingers unbuttoned her jeans, and then he lifted her and carried her back to the bed. With quick efficiency, he removed her boots and jeans and then his own.

She reclined on the pillows looking at him. He was the most extraordinary man she'd ever met. The wound where the bullet had grazed him was the only imperfection on a body that looked as if it could have been a sculpture. Instead of cold marble, though, his skin was a perfect bronze and it rippled across his muscles. Dark hair crossed his chest.

She was naked, but she felt no embarrassment or shyness. It was as if, at last, she'd stepped into her own destiny. Her body was languid, filled with a wantonness that surprised and delighted her. Never in her life had she considered taking an afternoon off from work for sex. Heaven forbid! In New York she'd barely had time to eat and sleep, much less enjoy the company of a man. Now, she couldn't think of a single thing she needed to be doing but this. Even Familiar had conspired to give her the afternoon alone with Hank.

"Ready for that shower?" he asked as he scooped her into his arms.

Before she could reply, he had her in the bathroom and had stepped under the spray with her in his arms. The water was the perfect temperature. She let it pound her face, streaming through her hair and splashing Hank's chest.

Setting her gently on her feet, he picked up the shampoo and lathered her hair. "I have to say, the only hair I've washed has been my horse's tail. Your hair is a lot softer."

She smiled under the spray of the shower. Some women wouldn't realize what a compliment Hank had paid her. He was a cowboy. Any comparison to his horse was solid gold.

"I don't kick, either," she said, nudging him gently with her heel. "But I could if provoked."

His arms slipped around her. "Then I'd have to teach you some manners. But I've always believed in gentling a horse—" his hands moved over her breasts "—showing them kindness—" he bent down to nuzzle her neck "—teaching them that touch is a pleasurable thing." His soapy hands moved over her stomach, his fingers gentle and caressing.

"Hank," she breathed as she turned in his arms and faced him. Their bodies were covered in soap and she moved against him, slick and wet. The water pounded down around them, and they were alone, the only two people alive.

The kiss became heated, hungry, as the water sprayed over them, rinsing away the soap. Hank led her out of the water and through the bathroom to the bed. She could feel his desire for her, and her own body felt leaden with need. She wanted him so badly she ached.

He put her in the bed and then straddled her. Slowly he leaned down for a long kiss. He was teasing her, building the fire inside her, making her want him beyond reason. Unable to take any more, she pulled him to her. They made love in the slanting afternoon light that turned the pale bedroom into shades of gold.

HANK SLIPPED ON his jeans and then his boots. Stephanie was still sleeping, the sunlight slipping through the blinds and highlighting her brown curls. She was the most beautiful woman he'd ever met.

They have taken a big step, sleeping together. One that couldn't be undone, no matter how uneasy he became. He stood in the doorway and watched Stephanie, wondering if his father had loved his mother the same way. Knowing that he had. He'd watched his dad dry up and become a thin replica of the man he'd once been. Jared Dalton had give up when his wife left him. Oh, he'd worked and done his best to raise his son, but the joy of life had left him and only a husk had remained.

Hank knew that he was running the same risk. They were men who loved only once, deeply. He'd begun to give his heart totally to Stephanie. His love was both a gift and a burden, because with it came the ability to destroy him, just as his mother had destroyed his father.

This was a woman he barely knew, a woman who'd left Texas once before without a backward glance. Even worse, she didn't pretend to be otherwise. When she'd asked him what would happen if she lost the farm, he'd blown off her question. Because he didn't want to think about what might happen then. Stephanie wouldn't be content to live on a working cattle ranch. That much he knew. He didn't have the acreage to support the types of cattle drives she was talking about. Merging the Running Z and McCammon Ranch was the way to achieve her dreams.

If she still had McCammon Ranch by Monday morning when the will would be officially probated.

She stirred, rolling over so that her hair fell across her face. He moved to the side of the bed and gently brushed her curls away. In her sleep she smiled and softly called his name.

He knew then that whatever the price he would pay, it was worth it. She was in his heart now, and only a fool would worry about the cost of such love.

He leaned down and kissed her cheek.

"Hank," she said, opening her eyes and smiling. "What time is it?"

"About five," he said. "I thought I'd go into the kitchen and rustle us up some supper."

"You can cook?" she frowned. "That's not one of the talents I remember going along with cowboys."

"It's a fine Western tradition. Beans. I can cook 'em any way you want 'em."

"Beans?" She wrinkled her nose. "What else?"

"Red beans."

She frowned.

"Black beans." He was trying hard not to laugh at her expression. "Pinto beans?" Pause. "Pork and beans?"

"How about some cole slaw and some grilled Portobello mushrooms?"

Now it was his turn to make a face. "I have to say, ma'am, that it's against the cowboy code to eat anything that grows in cow manure."

She laughed and threw a pillow at him. "Okay, Mr. Cowboy, cook some beans. Do your worst."

He gave a low bow. "Your wish is my command."

He was still chuckling when he went to the kitchen and started the process of making an omelet. It wasn't cowboy tradition for a man to cook, but he and Jared had learned the hard way that if they wanted something good to eat, they were going to have to learn to fix it themselves. The result had been they both developed certain specialties. It made the days of long hard work at least tolerable.

He started frying the bacon as he got eggs, cheese, red peppers and olives out of the refrigerator. He was busy at the cutting board when she walked into the kitchen, her hair still damp from the shower.

"Something smells wonderful. I'm starved," she said. "We forgot to eat the lunches Maizy packed for us."

"Food was the last thing on my mind when we got home," he said, chopping the red pepper.

She took a seat at the table, her gaze following him as he worked. He liked that she watched him.

"I thought Familiar would be home by now," she said, a hint of worry in her voice.

"Really? I just figured we'd pick him up in town. He's a guy, and one helluva detective," Hank said. He arched his eyebrows. "I doubted your stories at first, but I have to say, that cat is smarter than most humans."

"Don't let him hear you say that," Stephanie said. "He's already got a superiority attitude. If he hears us agreeing with him his head will swell so big he won't be able to get in the door."

He put a plate of sliced cheese in front of her. She took a thin slice and nibbled on it. "Hank, what do you think Rodney's role is in this?"

Hank scraped the onions and peppers into the frying pan with a sizzle. "I've thought about it a lot, and I'm afraid Rodney is being used."

She nodded. "Me, too. He seems crazy about Wanda, but I think she's just using him, and in the worst way. If she knew someone was going to burn the barn, she must have known his horses were in there, as well as mine."

"What's her angle?" Stephanie asked. "If she's romantically involved with Nate Peebles, how would it benefit him for the barn to burn? That's an expensive, valuable barn."

Hank cracked six eggs and began to whip them.

"That's a good point. But maybe frightening you away is more important than the value of an outbuilding."

"You think the same person was behind the snakes, too?"

"I do. That was his first attempt to send you packing. When it didn't work, he escalated. And quickly. That's something we should keep in mind. Peebles or whoever this is is willing to kill people. Albert and Emily." He poured the eggs in the skillet and turned to face her. "Maybe you and Familiar and Banjo should come stay at my place."

Stephanie shook her head. "I'm not leaving McCammon Ranch." Her eyes sparked with anger. "My family built this place. McCammon Ranch has been a going concern for five generations, and it isn't going to change now."

Stephanie was beautiful when she was asleep, and she was gorgeous when she was angry. He folded the omelet and put the spatula down so he could take her in his arms. "Then you have to let me stay here with you."

Her smile was naughty. "Just so long as you don't intend sleeping on the sofa again."

"Not on your life." He kissed her lightly and returned to the stove. He served the eggs on two plates with toast and jam and fresh peaches he'd sliced.

"Too bad Familiar isn't here," she said, putting a bite in her mouth.

"We'll have him with us in a matter of minutes."

I'm sitting here in the gathering dusk watching for Wanda Nell Hempstead, nee Washington, to come home from her job at the department store.

Here comes a car now, a compact in fair shape. It's turned into her driveway. Excellent. Wanda is home. I hope Stephanie and Hank have figured out where I am and are on the way. I'm starving to death. It was a noble action I took when I forwent lunch and decided to do some work. Now I'm ready for a little snack. Heck, I'm a working dick. I need more than a snack; I need a seven-course meal. With some crème brûlée for dessert.

I'm going to creep a little closer. Wanda has removed her dress and is standing in a garter belt, stockings and her undies. She has a great body. Too bad her expression is always so sour. She's talking on the telephone, standing in front of the air-conditioning vent. This heat is just killing me. No one has an open window, but the back door is cracked. Maybe I'll just slip inside and see what I can hear. And hopefully not get caught.

Her house is in need of a good cleaning. She has some nice things, but they don't seem to match. The table is an antique. The chair beside it is nouveau trash. It's as if she has no idea what's good and what isn't.

She's talking to another woman. I can hear her going on about the women who come in the department store thinking they're better than her. She wouldn't talk like that to a man.

I smell cigarette smoke, and now she's pacing. The tinkle of ice in a glass and something glugging out of a bottle. I just hope she doesn't come this way.

I'm going to peek around the corner and see what's

going on. She's taking off her stockings and putting on some shorts and tennis shoes. She's picking up her drink and heading toward me. Maybe to go out in the yard and garden some. The light is almost gone, though. She won't get many weeds pulled this evening.

From my perch by the door I can see the front yard, too, and I believe I saw Stephanie's rental drive by. She'll be looking for me. Now I need to scoot out of here without getting caught. I don't think Wanda is a cat person.

She's going outside, though. My curiosity is aroused. I do know the old saying about curiosity and cats. I believe it's highly superstitious. Cats may be more curious than other species, but I don't think the death rate is accelerated because of it. Then again, I've been in some real jams because I stuck my nose in the wrong place.

She's slipping past me in the dark entryway, and now she's outside, conveniently leaving the door cracked for me to slip out the same way I came in. But first, what is she doing? She's getting a shovel from the side of the house and she's hiking down the backyard with the shovel in hand. I didn't realize that her backyard fronts onto some kind of barren wilderness. Tumbleweed and dirt. She's headed out there in a pair of dang flip-flops.

She must know where she's going, because she doesn't seem to hesitate. All I can do is follow. And looks like we aren't going too far. About a hundred yards into the brush and she's stopping, putting some kind of small box or container down and beginning to dig. Not an easy job when one is wearing flip-flops.

The dirt is baked dry by the sun and hard as a rock,

but she's chipping away at it. Her arms are well-developed, something I hadn't noticed before in those dresses. Reminds me of some of those aerobic teachers—lean and fit. It's just a little odd for a salesclerk in a department store.

The hole is getting deeper. She's in about a foot now, and steady working at it. Whatever is buried must be small. I wish I could dart out to the road and flag down Stephanie and Hank. I can't chance missing what she digs up, though.

Okay, here it comes. It's a plastic bag and it looks like some kind of dead animal is in it. Something flat, like it's been run over. But why would she go to the trouble of burying a dead animal and then digging it up? I need to get closer to see what's going on. I'll ease over to this little dried-out shrub. And now I can see. It's a leather glove in the bag. Now she's putting the box down in the hole, putting the glove on top of it, and covering it all up again.

I think I'll make my presence known. That should give her something to think about. I'm stepping into the open and walking toward her with a few little meows to get her attention.

She's looking at me as if she's seen a ghost. She may have seen me with Stephanie and Hank, but she surely can't realize that I'm a private detective. Her reaction is interesting. She's raising the shovel and coming toward me. I think she means to smash me with the shovel.

Time to split! Like I said, she's a very physical woman. She's running after me with the shovel like she means business. Maybe she just has a hatred of cats that springs from some childhood issue. Who the heck cares! I'm making tracks and I hope that she doesn't follow me.

Oops! She swung the shovel. I darted out of the way, but she isn't playing around. She's panting and yelling, saying she's going to flatten me. I can see she means every word she's saying. My goodness, I'm back at the house. I'll dart under it and hit the front and see if I can't find a place to hide. She has to either come through the back gate or the house, and that should slow her down.

Whew! I made it to safety. She came out on the front porch and looked out, but she's breathing too hard to really pursue me. Now I have just one more thing to find an answer to. Why does Wanda Nell Hempstead hate cats so much?

Chapter Fourteen

Stephanie saw the black cat dart out into the middle of the road. She was far enough away to slow down. As the SUV came to a halt, she opened the door and Familiar darted into the front seat beside Hank.

"What's going on?" Hank asked the cat.

Familiar put his front paws on Stephanie's hand on the steering wheel and patted it lightly.

"A hand?" Hank asked as Stephanie drove away. "Something to do with a hand? Do you think Wanda hit him?"

Familiar blinked twice.

"He must have discovered something at her house." She turned right at the next corner and circled through town. "Maybe we should wait and see what she does?"

"Good idea," Hank said. Beside him, Familiar blinked twice. "The cat likes that idea, too. From the way he's winded, I'd say he was running from something, so we need to keep a sharp lookout."

"Was he running from Wanda?" Stephanie asked.

Familiar head-butted her chin.

"I think he agrees with that statement. So we can deduce that Familiar saw something he wasn't supposed to see that had to do with a hand, and then Wanda chased him." Stephanie slowed the SUV and pulled under the concealing branches of a cottonwood that grew beside the road. From where she was parked, she and Hank had a perfect view of Wanda's house.

She glanced at Hank. He was focused on Wanda's house and she had a moment to enjoy his profile. She knew the strength of his square jaw and the tenderness of his lips. There was the tiniest stubble on his cheeks. She didn't have to see it, because her face was still tingling from the slight rasp of his beard when he kissed her. She sighed.

"What are you thinking?" He reached over to touch her hand on the steering wheel.

"How handsome you are," she said.

"You must have me confused with some other cowboy," he said with a hint of teasing in his voice.

"No, I'm not confused. Maybe for the first time in my life, I'm not confused."

Familiar spun in a circle on the seat.

"I don't think the cat feels we should be talking romance when we're on a stakeout," Hank said, barely suppressing a laugh.

"Me-ow!" Familiar was emphatic.

"I have to agree with the cat," Stephanie said, "especially since Wanda's backing her car out." She put the SUV in Drive and waited until Wanda backed out and drove away. Stephanie let her get several blocks ahead before she followed.

"You act like you've done this before," Hank said.

"I had a client who worked on the set of *NYPD Blue*," she said. "He was into all the techniques of law enforcement. I guess I picked up some things just listening."

"You must have had a very exciting life in the big city."

Though his tone was casual, she understood what he was really asking. She reached across the seat and touched his thigh. "I had my share of excitement, but none of it can compare to this afternoon." She was amused to see a hint of a flush touch his cheeks.

"You're trying to flatter an old cowboy," he said, trying to brush it off.

"And you're playing the worn-out, old cowpoke card," she said, smiling, "but it's the truth. Believe it or not. That's up to you." She made a left following Wanda's car.

"Meow!" Familiar patted the speedometer, warning her to slow down. She was getting too close to Wanda.

"Where do you think she's going?" Stephanie asked. They were headed out of town in the direction of McCammon Ranch.

"Certainly not to the ranch. Unless she has a date with Rodney," Hank suggested.

"I'm not certain, but I think Rodney is backing off dating. He was torn up about the near fire. He's been rigging up boobytraps in the barn, in case anyone comes back to try to set another fire," Stephanie said. "I think we can put all of our suspicions about Rodney to rest."

"I agree," Hank said. "He loved your folks, Stephanie. I can see where he's fallen under the spell of Wanda, but not to the point that he would harm anyone, especially not Albert and Emily."

They passed the driveway to McCammon Ranch and kept going. When they'd traveled another few miles, Wanda turned off the highway onto Jim Ramsey Road.

"What the heck," Hank said. "If I didn't know better, I'd say she was headed toward Johnny and Jackie's house."

"Maybe she's friends with them," Stephanie said, disappointment in her voice. "She's about Jackie's age, maybe a year or two older."

Familiar stood up with his front paws on the dash and batted Stephanie's hand on the steering wheel.

"It's the hand thing," Stephanie said, stroking the cat's head as she drove. When Wanda took a left into the driveway of the Benton ranch, her car slowed, as if she suspected someone was following her. Stephanie drove right by the driveway and kept going.

"There's another driveway about two miles down the road. We can turn around and come back up here and wait," Hank suggested.

"So you don't think this is a social visit," Stephanie said. She felt a ripple of concern. The Bentons had been good to her aunt and uncle. They'd been considerate friends and picked up the slack when she was too busy with her career.

"We won't know unless we check it out," Hank said.

She turned around and killed her lights as she cruised

down the county road looking for a good place to park. The land was flat, and with the full moon slipping from behind clouds, there was a chance they might be seen. "What if she sees us?" she asked.

"We'll just have to risk it," Hank said. "If she's up to something, then she'll know someone is tailing her. If she isn't, she probably won't notice."

Sitting in the car, it was hard for Stephanie not to reach over and touch Hank. She felt so close to him. In fact, she felt as if he'd been part of her life for a long, long time. Her aunt Em would have said that was because they were destined to be together. Em had believed in destiny. She'd never doubted that she and Albert were meant to be together. As sad as their deaths were, it was a good thing they'd died at the same time. Neither one would have lived long after the other died.

Hank's gaze was like a touch, and she turned to look at him just as the moon came out from behind the clouds. He wanted to kiss her. She could read it in his eyes. She was about to lean over and kiss him when Familiar hissed.

She sat up and looked at the driveway. Something was coming down it. A vehicle, but the lights weren't on.

HANK COULD ALMOST TASTE Stephanie's lips. He hungered for her kiss. Familiar's hiss brought an end to a very pleasant fantasy.

Hank looked over to find Stephanie gripping the steering wheel as she focused on the driveway. He saw movement. A truck was coming down the driveway with its lights out. So, Wanda had known she was being followed. She'd undoubtedly alerted whoever was at the Benton ranch.

Johnny Benton. He'd known the man most of his life and never thought much about him one way or the other. Johnny had been a pillar of the local church and deeply involved with local political races, as had his wife, Jackie. She'd come to Pecos ten years before as a bride and had become very active in the community. Hank tried to remember the story he'd heard. Something about how Johnny had met Jackie in Dallas when he was there on business. It had been love at first sight, and the two had married after a whirlwind courtship of two months.

The vehicle turned from the driveway to the road. Hank could see a silhouette of a cowboy hat in the vehicle.

"It's not Wanda. It's Johnny," Hank said. "Don't turn our lights on. Just follow."

Stephanie nodded. She was as focused as she could be.

The truck picked up speed and headed back to town. When it was a hundred yards away, the driver turned the lights on. Stephanie waited and then followed, her lights still dark.

They went back to town, and Hank wasn't surprised when the truck stopped at Nate Peebles's home. Stephanie pulled to the curb a block away and waited. Their vision was partially blocked by a tallow tree, but there was no other place to park and wait. In spotty streetlight they could see a tall, lean man, his features shadowed by his hat, get out from behind the wheel.

"What would Johnny be doing here?" Stephanie whispered.

The man hurried up the sidewalk to the front door. He knocked once, hard, and the door immediately opened. In a moment he was inside.

"What the heck?" Stephanie said. She looked at Hank. "Do you think Johnny and Nate Peebles are in cahoots?"

Hank considered. "It sure looks that way." Something wasn't right though. "Where's Wanda, then?"

"At the ranch." Stephanie's eyes widened. "She's in it with Johnny. Johnny's not out of town in Austin. That's what Jackie said, remember? She said he wouldn't be back in time to ride in the rodeo, but that's a lie to cover up what he's doing tonight."

"That's right. So why is Wanda at the house?"

"She has to be part of it, somehow."

"Maybe," Hank said slowly. "Let's get out of here." As Stephanie pulled off, Hank noticed Familiar was looking out the window. It was as if he, too, were pondering the situation and the possible implications.

They drove back to McCammon Ranch. When they pulled into the yard, Stephanie was surprised to see Rodney sitting on the front porch waiting for them.

He stood when they drove up. "Miss Stephanie, I'm waiting on Doc Smith. I called him. Mirage is down with the colic."

"Mirage!" Stephanie was out of the SUV and running toward the barn. "How long?" she called out.

"About two hours. I gave her some Banamine and called the vet. He had an emergency, but he'll be here in about ten minutes.

Hank ran after Stephanie. Colic was the number one

killer of horses, and often times, there was little even a vet could do.

He found Stephanie in the horse's stall, kneeling beside the mare. She was resting comfortably, and Hank knelt beside her front leg and took a pulse.

"Should we get her up?" Stephanie asked.

Hank shook his head. "As long as she's not thrashing, we should let her rest." He took in some other details. "She's not sweaty, and her pulse isn't too elevated."

Stephanie rocked back on her heels. "What should we do?"

"Wait for the vet," he said, putting his hands on her shoulders. "That's all we can do."

The vet is a great idea, but I wish he'd get here. My humanoid, Dr. Peter Curry, has a mostly small-animal practice, but I've heard him consult with experts on large animals. Colic is something he knows a lot about. I sure wish Peter were with me now.

From what I remember of his conversations, some of the causes of colic are overeating, bad food, getting too hot, a change in the barometric pressure, anxiety, stress, you get the picture. It can be anything and everything. But I'm wondering if this is a case of natural colic or something caused by man. I just want to check around and see if I can find anything unusual in the feed room.

Let's see, those are oats, sweet feed, alfalfa pellets, bran, all of this looks normal to me. In the supplements I see some electrolytes, trace minerals and a supplement for Mirage's hooves. I'm not psychic, but I know it belongs to Mirage because her name is written on it. Wait a minute, the hoof supplement looks like two different things have been put in the same container.

I'm going to get Hank in here. He doesn't want to leave Stephanie, but if I apply a little more claw in his tush, he'll get the message. Ah, he's standing up and looking at me. He's not happy, but he's following me into the feed room. He's examining the bucket of supplements, and he's drawing the same conclusion that I drew. Someone has tampered with the supplements.

DOC SMITH EXAMINED the bucket of supplements. "I'll take some samples, but it looks to me like some diuretic agent." He'd combated Mirage's illness with a drip to get fluids into her and some oil and an antacid to help her stomach. She was on her feet and looking much perkier. Stephanie stroked her sleek neck and gave her another piece of carrot.

"Do you have any idea who could have done this?" Doc asked. His gaze shifted to Rodney, who frowned and shook his head.

"Anyone could have come in here during the day while I was out with the cows," Rodney said. "It doesn't matter who did this, it's my fault. I should have been watching things more carefully. I knew someone was up to no good."

"Rodney, it isn't your fault. Had I been feeding, I wouldn't have looked at the hoof supplement. I would have given Mirage the same thing you did." Stephanie knew she had to relieve his guilt. Rodney might not be the brightest lamp in the house, but he loved the horses more than his own life.

"Dang it! Who's doing this?" Rodney's frustration was apparent in his voice. "If they want to fight, let 'em come on and fight, but leave the innocent animals out of it."

Stephanie put her arm around his shoulders as best she could. "Mirage is going to be okay. That's what matters."

"Miss Stephanie, I've been racking my brain. It could be anyone who knows a bit about horses. Anyone."

It was true. Stephanie knew that. The barn was wide-open, as were the farmhouse and all the outbuildings. Anyone could have tampered with the horse's feed. "Maybe we need to get a lock on the feed room door," she said.

"I'll have this analyzed," Doc said, "but if we can find out who's doing this, I'd like to see them prosecuted."

"Legal prosecution is going to come second to what I have in mind for them," Hank assured him.

Doc pulled Hank to the side and motioned for Stephanie to join them. "I had a rush on that DNA test," he said. "My college roommate works in the lab, and he did it special for me. It's a match between the blood on the glove and the scraping we took from the cat's paw."

"You're certain?" Stephanie asked.

"Very certain." Doc looked down at his boots. "There's something else," he said.

Stephanie didn't know the veterinarian well, but she

realized he knew something important. It was his high opinion of Hank that made him willing to talk.

"What?" she asked.

"Someone came into the clinic today with a scratched face."

"Who?" Hank asked.

"Johnny Benton," he said. "Johnny said his wife's cat clawed him. That might be the truth. They have a cat, and she's a real temperamental creature. Could be, though, that he got scratched right here in this barn. I can't say, but I figured you should know."

"Johnny Benton." Stephanie felt as if she'd been tapped on the head with a hammer. Everywhere they turned it seemed that he showed up.

"He came in for some flea medication, but then he hedged around asking if I had some antibiotic ointment."

Stephanie nodded. That would make sense. If he was the man in the drugstore, he didn't buy anything to treat his scratch marks. Once he left the drugstore when Familiar had spotted him, he'd gone to the vet's. "Did you give him anything for the wounds?" she asked.

Doc shook his head. "I can't treat people. I told him he should get a tetanus and have someone clean the wounds. I got the idea he wasn't going to listen to me, though."

"Thanks, Doc," Hank said. "I owe you."

"You two just be careful. I've known Johnny Benton all my life. I always wondered what Albert saw in him, because he sure set a sight in Johnny."

Stephanie remembered well how much her uncle had

wanted her to marry Johnny. She hadn't been able to, though. She simply hadn't felt the kind of love necessary to sustain a marriage.

She felt Doc Smith's gaze on her and when she met it, he smiled. "I know your uncle had planned on you marrying Johnny. I have to say I was relieved when I heard you'd packed up and gone to New York."

Stephanie frowned. "Why do you say that?"

"Johnny isn't the man he pretends to be," Doc said. He took a deep breath. "I've learned through life to judge a man by how he treats his animals. Johnny is a callous man. He's ruled by his desire for money. Jackie has had a sad life. Every time I see her she's always talking about how she wanted children and Johnny didn't. She's never come out and said it, but the clear implication is that he has a mean streak. A few times she's had bruises that she couldn't explain. I got the impression that maybe he hurt her."

Stephanie thought back to those long-ago years when she was in high school and Johnny courted her. He'd never been anything but solicitous and kind. Not once had he raised his voice to her or even tried to pressure her into having sex with him before the marriage.

At the time it hadn't occurred to her that his behavior was bizarre. She didn't love him, so she had no desire for physical intimacy. But he'd claimed to love her. He'd asked her to marry him. Yet he hadn't been interested in sex.

"Stephanie, are you okay?" Hank was beside her, his fingers lightly grasping her arm and supporting her.

"I was just thinking," she said. "Johnny Benton was after McCammon Ranch all along. He never really cared about me. He wanted the ranch and everything that came with it. I was just the route to get it."

She felt angry. What would her life have been like if she'd married him?

Doc nodded. "I wouldn't put it past Johnny."

"But this went on for two years. He was with me all the time, always at the ranch. Not one single time did I ever see him lose his temper."

"Is that a normal reaction?" Doc asked.

Of course it wasn't. But she'd never looked beyond the surface of Johnny Benton's conduct. Now that Doc had pointed it out, though, she realized that she'd never had an argument with Johnny. He was as smooth and polished as glass. Whatever emotions he might have been feeling were carefully concealed.

"He's a con," she said. "And the whole time I've been gone he's been conning my aunt and uncle." A terrible thought struck her. "Do you think he conned them into changing the will?"

Doc tilted his head. "Let me just say one thing. Your uncle Albert was dead-set on keeping McCammon Ranch as a working ranch. He was surprised to see me when I went out to vaccinate the cows. He didn't say much, just that he wasn't expecting me. It never occurred to me to tell him that I was stumped that Peebles had sent me out there. I wish I'd told him then and there."

Stephanie wished that, too, but how would Doc have

known? She shook her head. "Some things are beginning to make sense. Now all we have to do is prove it. Before Monday, when the will is read."

She looked at Hank. "I have a terrible feeling if we don't have the evidence to contest the will Nate Peebles has on Monday, we aren't going to get a second chance."

Hank nodded. "I'm afraid you're right. The more I think about it, remember that bulldozer that I found. It wasn't to take the fences down. It was to raze the farmhouse. I believe they intended to make it impossible for you to stay at the ranch."

"I'm afraid you're right, and once Peebles has the court decision, he'll destroy everything on the ranch that he can."

Doc patted her shoulder. "You don't look like the kind of lady who'll let that happen, and I know Hank isn't that kind of man."

"Meow!"

Doc glanced down at the cat. "Something tells me this isn't that kind of cat, either. Now let's check that mare one more time before I have to get home and get some rest."

They all three moved back to the stall where Rodney was washing Mirage's face with a cool sponge. "She's feeling better," Rodney said, relief evident in his face. "I think she's going to be fine."

Doc examined her gums and checked her respiration and gut noises. "I agree with your diagnosis, Rodney. I'll get these supplements checked and be in touch."

"Doc, would you mind standing by tomorrow night at the rodeo?" Stephanie asked.

"That won't be a hardship at all," he said, grinning. "I've got two teams lined up for the team penning."

Chapter Fifteen

Stephanie sat in the swing under the huge oak in the backyard and watched the sun rise. Her eyes were itchy with fatigue, but she couldn't sleep. She and Hank had made love and afterward, feeling safe and secure, she'd fallen into a deep sleep for an hour. Anxiety about Mirage had awakened her, and she'd checked on the horse every hour throughout the night. The mare was doing fine. Unable to fall back asleep, Stephanie had come outside, hoping not to awaken Hank. Now the sun was coming up over the horizon and soon it would be time to start the process of beginning the rodeo.

Everything was in perfect order. The animals were ready, Sonja and Kimberly assured her. Concessions were arranged; the mayor had called up and offered to open the rodeo with a brief talk about the history of the rodeo in Pecos. It would seem that the entire town was behind her in this effort. But someone wasn't. Someone had tried to burn her horses and colic her mare. She and

Hank were going to have to be vigilant. Thank goodness Familiar was helping.

She went to the back door and let Banjo come out with her. He was feeling better. Doc had checked his leg and said it seemed to be mending perfectly. As soon as the cast was off and he regained his strength, he'd be able to return to herding. It was killing the dog to be shut inside. Until he healed, though, there was nothing else to do. She didn't want to risk further injury even if Banjo didn't understand why he had to be kept calm.

The dog followed her back to the swing and eased down at her feet. Even injured he'd do his best to protect her. She stroked his head as she thought.

There was no doubt that Nate Peebles was involved in trying to steal the ranch. Now, she could add Johnny Benton, maybe Jackie, to the list, as well as Wanda Hempstead. But how did they all fit in it together? Nate Peebles was the only one who stood to gain anything financially. The will—the fake will—listed him as the sole beneficiary. Why would Johnny be involved in something like that where he had nothing to gain?

But what was Johnny doing with Nate Peebles?

None of it made any sense. Stephanie's head was spinning. Banjo gave a low whine and she instantly tensed. She looked up to see Familiar easing toward her. Obviously he couldn't sleep, either. She patted her lap and he jumped up, giving her a few head-butts and lots of purrs.

"I'm worried, big guy," she whispered. "I'm afraid someone is going to try to destroy the rodeo. A good lawsuit would accomplish that, and Nate Peebles is just the man to initiate something like that."

Familiar continued to purr. He put his paw on her face and patted her gently. She couldn't help but smile at him. He was one smart cat.

"Okay, let's go inside and make some coffee." She kept the cat in her arms as she and Banjo walked slowly back to the ranch house. She'd just turned the coffeepot on when the phone rang. She picked it up and felt her spirits rise as she heard Sonja's recounting of the entries.

"We have thirty teams for team penning, twenty entries in the barrels and fifteen rides for the broncs and bulls. We'll have to cull it down to twelve, but I think we can manage that," Sonja said with excitement. "And everyone has been interested in watching a demonstration of my training skills. In fact, one man is going to bring an unbroken three-year-old mare. I'm going to demonstrate throughout the whole rodeo some of the training techniques I use, and I'll ride her before the night is over, all without frightening her or hurting her in any way."

"That's worth the price of admission, Sonja." Stephanie wanted to hug the trainer and intended to so do as soon as she saw her in person.

"I try to give these demonstrations as often as possible. Once people understand that force or brutality isn't necessary, most horse owners are willing to try my methods."

"This rodeo is going to make a big difference, for a lot of people and animals," Stephanie said. "Thank you."

"Kimberly and I are on our way to Maizy's to get some breakfast. We'll see you when you get to town."

As Stephanie hung up the phone, she looked up to see Hank standing in the doorway. His hair was deliciously rumpled. She walked over to him and lightly kissed his lips, running her hands through his hair. "I was hungry for breakfast until I saw you," she said, thinking of the big bed and how nice it would be to share it with Hank.

"Me-ow!" Familiar was indignant. He walked over to Stephanie and swatted her bare leg.

"Ouch," she said, hopping on one leg. "What was that for?"

Hank laughed. "Familiar is telling you to straighten up. I think he's shocked at your conduct."

She flushed and then laughed. "Familiar is right, though, we need to tend to business."

"The rodeo is our priority today."

She looked down at the tile floor. "Maybe I bit off more than I can chew." She couldn't help that she was worried. Any number of things could go wrong.

"That's not the self-confident city girl I thought I knew," Hank said as he put his arms around her. Familiar rubbed against her ankles, purring.

"I guess with the support of the two guys—"

She was interrupted by the sound of Banjo barking at the door.

"Excuse me, my *three* guys, I can't go wrong."

Hank squeezed her tightly. "That's right, cowgirl. You can't go wrong with us behind you."

She was smiling as she went to get ready to head to town.

THE DAY HAD FLOWN BY in a series of minor emergencies. Hank had worked on the gear for the broncs and bulls, rewired the lights, repaired the PA system, found a barrel for the rodeo clown, tied the numbered collars on the team penning cattle and, finally, got into his chaps for the bull riding. He'd drawn the fourth ride on Little Mister, maybe the roughest bull in the herd. Little Mister was small and compact, a fact that seemed to give him more punch. It was going to be one heck of a ride.

Hank walked up to the chute where two of his hands had already tied a strap around the bull's withers. In some rodeos another strap, tightly cinched around the bull's flanks, pinched the animal's private parts to encourage bucking. Stephanie disapproved of such tactics, and Hank agreed. Either the bull enjoyed bucking or he didn't. There was no need to induce bucking with pain.

Junior and Wesley hovered over the tall pen as Hank eased his legs around the bull.

"I'm sorry for the day you got down in the gulch and I had to drag you out," Hank said to Little Mister as he slipped his hand under the rope and got a good grip. He had a vivid memory of the bull bellowing with fear and indignation as Hank had slipped the rope around his body and used his horse Rio to help pull the young bull out of the steep gulch before the storm broke and a flash flood drowned the animal.

"Apologizing now won't do a bit of good," Junior

said. "Littler Mister remembers the way you manhandled him, and he was just a yearling. Now he's a big man and it's time for payback."

"He would've died if I hadn't rescued him," Hank argued. "He should be grateful, not vengeful."

"Tell it to Little Mister," Junior said. "You ready?"

Hank had his legs on the bull and he could feel the eighteen hundred pounds of muscle and bone bowing up beneath him.

"I don't know if I'll ever be ready for this," Hank answered, "but turn him loose!"

Junior threw the gate open and the bull jumped into the arena in a straight-legged sunfish that made Hank's head snap back. He had a blurred vision of the stands. They seemed full of people in brightly colored clothes—a montage of colors as he spun. The bull twisted, throwing his head down and his back feet almost straight up in the air. It was all Hank could do to hang on.

His legs were off the bull and wide apart, and he could feel the brim of his hat touching the bull's back as Little Mister whirled and jumped.

Hank felt as if he'd been riding the bull for half his lifetime. His arm was numb from the shock of trying to hang on to the bucking, twisting mass of muscle.

Little Mister leapt straight into the air and came down with his back arched. He jumped to the left, back to the right, up in the air again and ducked his head so low that Hank saw only the ground rising up to meet his face. He managed to jerk his hand free of the rope around the bull's withers and used his arms to push himself clear of the bull.

He landed soft in the dirt and rolled. He came up, winded, but uninjured. He could hear the roar of the crowd, but he had not heard the eight-second bell. He didn't have a winning ride, but the crowd was cheering enthusiastically anyway.

"Hank! Watch out!"

He heard the voice of the rodeo clown from behind, and he rolled quickly—just before Little Mister's horns slammed into the ground beside him.

The bull's behavior was purely vindictive, and Hank rolled again, just before the bull made another attempt to gore him. Hank knew he had to get to his feet and fast.

"Over this way, Hank!" The rodeo clown ran past him right in front of the bull, trying to draw Little Mister's attention away, but the bull wasn't distracted. He had eyes only for Hank, who had gained all fours and was scrambling away.

Hank felt the ground shake and knew Little Mister was charging him. The clown's barrel was only a few feet away and he dove for it, curling inside just as the bull struck the barrel with such force that Hank was afraid it would shatter.

The fact that he wasn't visible would confuse the bull for a few moments, but Hank knew it wouldn't last. Bulls could smell, like all other animals, and soon Little Mister would sniff him out. He heaved his body to the left and began to roll the barrel. He heard the crowd scream, and he wondered what was going on. In a moment he saw a flash of black and silver. Rio! His horse was in the arena, but how? He craned out of the barrel and saw Stephanie riding Rio right toward the bull.

His heart thudded painfully, but he also felt pride. She was one woman. After years in the big city, she hadn't lost her ability to ride.

Stephanie gave a shrill whistle and used the lariat he'd hung on his saddle horn to slap the bull on the rump. Little Mister bellowed with anger and trotted back toward the gates where Junior and several other men were waiting to herd him into the holding pen.

Hank crawled out of the barrel to standing applause. When Stephanie wheeled Rio and rode toward him, he grabbed her extended hand and pulled himself up behind the saddle. Mounted together, they rode out of the arena to hoots and whistles.

"Thanks for the rescue," he said as soon as she stopped the horse. He didn't dismount. He was quite comfortable with his arms around her. She was hot, and he could feel her heart hammering.

"What's the issue between you and that bull?" she asked.

"It's a long story, but I didn't think Little Mister would hold a grudge for the past two years."

"He wanted a piece of you," she said, turning slightly. She kissed him, a kiss of desire and relief and joy. "I was terrified," she whispered.

He slid to the ground and then lifted her from the saddle. "I've been in more comfortable positions," he said. "Let's watch the rest of the riders."

Together they walked to the rail and watched as the last two bull riders took a turn. A twenty-year-old boy named Mitch Walch rode Lusty for the full time and ended up with the win. Hank and Stephanie applauded as he took a bow.

"I don't know that I want to do that every Friday night," he said, rolling his shoulders. "I may not be any wiser, but I am a little older."

"Thanks for doing it this week. I think the rodeo is a success, so far."

"And the team penning is still to come. Speaking of which, I'd better get over to check the cattle. I want it all to run like clockwork."

She stopped him with a hand on his arm. Before he could say anything, she kissed him again. "I think if kissing were a competitive sport, we could win."

"We already have," he said as he tipped his hat and walked away whistling.

While Hank and Stephanie are busy playing Annie Oakley and Wild Bill Hickok, I've been watching the crowd. There must be at least five hundred people here, which isn't bad for an unadvertised event. Most of them seem like ordinary folk out for an evening of fun and entertainment.

The exception is Jackie Benton. She's been at her horse trailer all evening, and a succession of men have stopped by, including Junior and Wesley. They had a quick conversation and before I could get over there, the wranglers were moving on. Could have been a casual greeting, but I didn't get to hear what was said. I just

*don't like it. After last night, I get the impression that
Jackie Benton is someone we have to watch.*

*She's saddling her gelding. I find it strange that her
husband isn't here with her, since he's in town. Maybe
he doesn't want anyone to see his scratched face.*

*Now Jackie's getting ready to ride into the arena
and warm up. The barrel racing is over and it's time for
team penning, the last event of the night.*

*I'll be glad when this day is over. It's been a big suc-
cess, but horses just aren't my thing. Sure they're beautiful to watch running, but try sitting on one for an hour
or more. It feels like my brains have been bounced to
the bottom of my toes.*

*I've been thinking about the wounds on Johnny Ben-
ton's face. The blood samples from my claws matched
the blood on the glove in the collapsed barn. And Wanda
was burying a second glove, perhaps the mate to the one
we found.*

*Now, if we could get a DNA sample from Johnny
Benton and have it tested, if it matches the other two
samples, we'd have our man without a doubt. The question is, how to get that sample when the man is never
around where he's supposed to be.*

*What I need to find out is if his wife is a willing par-
ticipant in his scheme or if she's someone who's been
pulled into it because she's married to a villain.*

*Well, well, looks like Wanda Hempstead is a cowgirl,
too. She's riding up on a paint. It would seem that she
and Jackie have had a falling out, because Jackie is
frowning at her and seems to be telling her to leave. I*

guess I'll saunter a little closer. I have to be careful, though. Wanda has already tried to brain me with a shovel. I don't want her to have a second chance at me.

I guess I'll just have to tail Wanda when she leaves. They're calling the lineup for the first few rides and Stephanie and Hank are on the third team. I should mosey over there and see how cooperative the cows are because that's where Wanda is heading. Jackie is on the third team, too, but she's riding in the opposite direction. There's something about this that just doesn't sit well with me.

Yikes! Wanda has spotted me, and she's headed my way at a full gallop. I have to find a place to hide! Under the bleachers. Make way for a cat! Whew! She almost trampled me to death, and it was deliberate. There's no doubt now that she recognizes me and has every intention of killing me if she can. I just can't help but take that a little personally, and it's going to be my pleasure to put Miss Wanda Hempstead behind bars for a long, long time.

STEPHANIE HEARD the commotion near the spectator stands but she was busy at the gate, trying to get the first team of penners into the arena and ready to ride. People were hollering, but she couldn't see anything.

Hank was at the far end of the arena settling the herd of thirty cows. They were young and inexperienced, and it was going to take some good riding to pen any of them. Another herd of sixty cows were in a holding pen on the far side of the arena.

As soon as she had the gate closed, she waved to the announcer to hold off for a moment. She noticed a young boy standing by her and gave him ten dollars to man the gate while she checked on a few things. As hard as she'd prepared for the night, there were jobs she hadn't counted on filling. Opening and closing the gate as teams rode in and out of the arena was one of the things she'd forgotten.

She jogged around the arena toward the place where the spectators stood. Several of them pointed behind the stands. Whatever it was, she had to check it out. She was almost there when Familiar ran out from under the stands and leapt into her arms.

"Hey, that lady tried to kill your cat," a young girl said. "She rode her horse right at the cat."

"What lady?" Stephanie asked, feeling an instant surge of anger. What kind of person would try to run down a cat?

"I don't know her. Blond hair. Chin-length. Major attitude, and she was looking right at the cat when she rode toward him."

"Thanks," Stephanie said, stroking Familiar's head. "Which way did she go?"

"Toward the cattle pens," the girl said and turned back to face the arena. "They're starting the team penning."

Stephanie held Familiar in her arms as she walked back to the announcer's stand. As she climbed the steps, she held the cat to her chest, glad he hadn't been injured.

"You stay up here," she told Familiar as she put him in an empty seat beside the announcer. "Keep an eye on him, Matt."

"Sure thing, Miss Stephanie. What's a cat doing up here anyway?"

"He's my mascot," she said and thought Familiar would hiss at her. "He's very special to me."

"Hey, what's going on with the cows?" John asked, a note of concern in his voice as he pointed across the arena.

Stephanie felt her heart begin to pound. The young cows for the team penning were mooing and milling at the end of the arena, but it was the cattle in the holding pen that John was talking about. A cloud of dust was rising. The cattle had been there all morning, and most had seemed content enough. Now, though, they were stampeding in the small enclosure. As Stephanie watched, a roar went up from the crowed as one cow smashed into the sides of the pen. It started a panic, and all of the cows began to bump and ram into each other. Their frightened cries had begun to draw the attention of the entire arena.

"Hank's down there," Stephanie said, instantly concerned. "I'll be back. Don't start the penning until I give you the signal," she called as she clattered down the steep stairs. She vaulted the railing of the arena and ran full speed, ignoring the spectators as they slowly rose to their feet for a better view of what was happening.

"Hank," she whispered his name as she ran. She didn't call out to him. She was using all of her lung capacity to get to him. As she covered the distance, she heard the cows grow even more distressed. One, in particular, sounded as if it were dying.

Several men had gathered around the railing, but no one was making any effort to stop whatever was happening.

"What's wrong?" she asked Junior as she pushed him aside. "What's wrong?"

"The cows just started going nuts," Junior said. "We can't see anything for all the dust they stirred up."

"Where's Hank?" she asked, feeling her dread increase.

"We haven't seen him," Junior said. "He's riding in the team penning. Maybe he's somewhere saddling up."

"He came over here." Stephanie thought her heart would pound out of her chest. The cattle were insane. They were slamming into each other and the wooden rails. Some of them sounded as if they'd injured themselves. "Hank's in there somewhere," she said, and as soon as the words left her lips, she knew they were true.

Chapter Sixteen

Stephanie used her boot to try to break the lock on the gate to the cattle pen. She kicked the jammed lock once, twice, then a third time with everything she had. It wouldn't budge! The cattle were going to injure themselves—or someone else—if they weren't freed from the packed enclosure.

She gave the lock another hard kick to no avail and began to climb the railing.

"Miss Stephanie, don't go in there," Junior said. "The cows are panicked. They'll stomp you to death."

Stephanie ignored him and vaulted the rail. The cattle had gone completely insane. She knew they could trample her to death and never even realize it. As if to prove that point, a small red calf rammed against her so hard she felt the air leave her lungs. She caught her breath and grabbed the calf. It was terrified and struggled, bellowing in fear. Stephanie penned it against the fence so that it wouldn't fall beneath the hooves of the other cows. In their panic, they would step on it and kill it.

"Junior!" she called, hanging on to the calf for all she was worth. "Help me."

With some reluctance Junior climbed the fence and came to help her lift the small calf out of the frenzied herd. "Get this one out. Just turn him loose in the arena," she said.

She turned back to face the herd. The panic showed no signs of abating, and the churning hooves had raised a thick cloud of dust. Hank was in there somewhere and she had to find him. She also had to discover what had frightened the cows so badly. They'd been at the arena all afternoon and had shown no signs of fear.

She untied her kerchief and retied it over her nose to help cut down on the dust and another acrid odor that stung her eyes and nostrils. Through squinted eyes, she made her way around the edge of the enclosure, desperate for a glance of Hank. He had to be in there somewhere, and he had to be okay. If he was hurt…she couldn't bear to think about it.

Once she'd circled half the perimeter without seeing him, she knew she had to go into the cows. They were whirling and spinning, still without any reason she could detect. As she started forward, moving slowly, the stinging in her eyes got more intense and she caught the sharp odor again. Fire. The thought shot through her like an arrow. The only place a fire could start would be near the north side of the pen. There were several old, unused holding pens that had been filled with debris. That had to be where the fire was.

She angled back to the perimeter and raced toward

the north. She could smell the fire stronger now. She understood the cows' panic, and when she passed Rodney beginning to climb over the fence, she stopped him.

"Call the fire department. Get some men and some water."

"Fire!" Rodney smelled it to. "I'll get some help."

"Get someone to get an ax and open the gate to the arena and let the cows out of the pen," she said. "Hurry!"

Rodney was gone in the cloud of dust that seemed to envelop her. Where was Hank? She had to find him. She ran to the north end of the pen. Through the dust she saw the flames licking at the railing. The fire was moving slowly down the dry old timbers of the stock enclosures.

"Hank!" She called his name, hoping that he could hear her and would respond. "Hank!"

Beside her a flash of black disappeared among the hooves of the cows. "Familiar!" She made a grab for the cat but missed him. "Come back!" She felt frustration and fear squeeze her heart.

There was no sign of the cat or Hank.

HANK FELT THE GROUND shaking all around him as he slowly regained consciousness. His head was throbbing. His memory was vague, but he remembered enough to know that the cows had panicked and stampeded him. He saw a cow's hoof come down only inches from his head and realized he had to move, but not too fast. The cows were doing their best not to step on him, but if he panicked them worse than they already were, anything could happen.

He got to his feet with deliberate movements. All around him the cows were running into each other and bellowing with fear. He caught the scent of fire on the dusty air and realized what was going on. Someone had set a fire, hoping the cows would panic, just as they were doing. He wasn't certain if the goal had been to injure him or to finish off the rodeo by possibly injuring the livestock and any luckless spectators.

In all the dust he was disoriented, but he slowly began to move, knowing that eventually he'd make it to a fence, if he wasn't run down.

"Hank!" He heard Stephanie calling him, but he couldn't tell what direction her voice came from.

"Over here," he called out, realizing he sounded weak.

"Hank!" she called again.

"I'm here!" He called, regaining his strength with every second. "Stay at the fence!" The last thing he needed was for her to try to move into the whirling cows.

"Are you hurt?" she called.

"I'm okay." He was getting closer to her. "There's a fire."

"Junior is getting help," she said, relief evident in her voice.

He saw her, a kerchief tied over the lower part of her face against the dust and steadily increasing smoke. In the distance he heard the sound of sirens. He guessed it was the fire truck and hoped his assumption was correct.

There was something he had to tell Stephanie. First, though, he had to get out of the cows. He moved another few yards and stopped. The herd seemed to be thinning, but he couldn't be certain.

Through the dust and smoke he saw Stephanie searching for him, her face furrowed with anxiety. When she finally saw him, she pulled the kerchief from her face and called his name. The smile that lit her face was the prettiest thing he'd ever seen. Her feelings were written large on her face, and he had no doubt that he would risk everything for her.

"Are you hurt?" She rushed up to him and put her arm around his waist as if she meant to help him to safety.

"I'm okay," he said.

She glanced at his shirt and he realized that blood had soaked the front of his shirt. "One of the cows took a little hide off my ear," he said. "Doc Smith always says that an ear wound is bad for bleeding."

"I'll say." They were at the rail, but she didn't loosen her grip on him.

"Need some help?" Junior and Wesley appeared. They both jumped the fence and hurried up to Hank. "Man, we were worried."

Hank looked at them. "I'm okay. What about the cows?"

"They're moving out into the arena, like Miss Stephanie told us to do," Junior said. "Once they get away from here and realize they're not hurt, they'll be fine."

"Good," Hank said.

He looked beyond the wranglers at the fire truck. The

firemen were quickly dousing the flames in the debris pile. No serious damage to the arena had been done. The danger had been in the stampeding cows—either they would be hurt or someone would be hurt trying to control them. And it had almost happened that way.

Hank shifted his focus to his two hands. Junior's sun-weathered face was pulled into a frown, and Wesley was as taciturn as ever as he watched the firemen work. Junior and Wesley had been on the scene, but it had been Stephanie who'd risked her life to search for him. Junior had worked for him for two years and Wesley for five. It was hard to suspect someone who worked beside you every day, but Hank had come to the realization that everyone was a potential suspect.

"Are you sure you're okay?" Junior asked, a frown touching his face. "What happened to your ear?"

"When the cows stampeded, I got trampled," Hank said casually. "Any idea who might have set the fire?"

Junior's frown deepened. "I didn't see anyone back there around the cows. Did you, Wesley?"

Wesley shook his head. "I was watching those girls ride their horses. I wasn't paying much attention to the cows."

"Me, too," Junior said. "Rodney's girl, Wanda, was riding her paint over here, warming up." He looked down at the ground. "I guess I was paying more attention to her than anything else."

Hank sighed. "I want to talk to both of you later."

"Sure. We're going to see about the cows."

The two men took off and Hank felt Stephanie's gaze on him. She put her hand on his arm, her grip warm and strong. "Before we talk, I have to find Familiar. He went tearing off into the middle of the cows to make sure you were okay."

Hank nodded. "Let's do it."

"You sit this one out, cowboy," Stephanie said, putting a hand on his chest. "I can find Familiar and then I'll report back here."

"I'm not an invalid," Hank said. "I'll get the team penning started. The fire, the stampede—" he waved his hand "—the whole thing is designed to make the rodeo fail. You can't afford to let them destroy you on the first night. We have to keep the rodeo on schedule."

He could see she didn't like his plan, but she nodded. "You're right. Are you sure you're up to it?"

"I'm okay. I just have a dull headache, and a throbbing ear. I might have to let my hair grow out for a week or two." He smiled to reassure her.

"As soon as I find the cat, I'll be up there to help," she said.

"Right."

"Before you go back to the stands, you might want to consider changing your shirt," she said, pointing to the blood.

"I'll take care of it." She was looking at him with such worry that he touched her cheek. "I'm fine. I promise."

"Are you?" she asked. "Hank, nothing is more important than you. Not the ranch or the rodeo or anything. None of it would be worth having without you. I guess that's what I've come to realize."

He'd never heard sweeter words. "Well, we've got a

fight to hang on to the rodeo and the ranch, but it's a fight we're going to win. No little bump on the head is going to change that."

Where are the humanoids when I need them? Almost all of the cows are out of the pen, the fire is out and now I can begin to do my work. There's not a chance any footprints will be left in the dirt after that stampede, but I hope I can find something.

It would seem to me that the firebug came from the back of the arena here. There's a rutted road, but it's certainly passable. I don't detect any new tracks, though. The light is not good here, so I'll come back in the morning and recheck. Yes, felines have superior night vision to humanoids, but even a cat has difficulty seeing the minute details of footprints in sand.

I'd be willing to bet that the firebug came on foot— or on horseback. Wanda Hempstead gets my vote as the most likely candidate. She was in the vicinity riding her paint. Warming up. A likely story. She'd already warmed the horse up by trying to kill me.

The cows are clearing out, and I see that the volunteer firemen are rolling up the hoses. Thank goodness the fire was never serious. I don't believe it was intended to be. It was meant to do exactly what it did— stampede the herd. At first the attacks were focused on Stephanie, but whoever is doing it has quickly begun to see Hank as an equal threat. That's interesting.

I'm going to have to attach myself to one of the humanoids so I'll be on the scene when the next attack occurs. If I'd been with Hank—instead of confined to the announcer's stand—I'd have the culprit rounded up by now.

No sense crying over spilt milk. Speaking of milk, I'd certainly like some icy cold cow product right this minute. It's amazing that with all of these cows on the property not a single one of them gives milk. No, these are the fleet of foot cows—the ones who evade capture in the small pen near the front of the arena.

I hear Hank calling for the teams and giving a brief explanation of what happened, all downplayed. And here comes Stephanie, looking for me. Sigh. I wish she'd stop worrying about me. I need to be able to do my job, but she's as protective as the proverbial mother hen.

Now that I have her attention, she's a bit calmer, and she's following me, just as I hoped. We're headed to the still smoldering pile of debris that someone deliberately torched. There has to be some evidence of the perpetrator. It's my job to find it.

I'll work the scene in a grid pattern, starting at the outside and working in. Well, well, the first interesting bit of physical evidence. A hoofprint. And not a cow. This is a horse that's been shod, just like Wanda Hempstead's horse, and yes, about sixty other horses here. The tracks lead up to the exterior of the pen. It's hard to tell after that, because the fire truck has been here, along with about fifteen men.

Stephanie is right with me. She's had a rough night. Heck, she's had a rough week. When no one is watching, I see the sadness pass over her face. No matter how

*much in love with Hank she is, there's still the loss of
her aunt and uncle and the way life was at McCammon
Ranch. I see her sometimes looking out the kitchen window or just pausing when she's walking across the
place, and I know that's what she's remembering.
There's an edge of anger there, too, that someone stole
all of this from her.*

*Someone, or several someones, came onto this ranch
and weakened the structure of the barn so that it would
fall on her aunt and uncle. I think in a lot of ways,
Stephanie hasn't fully processed all of that. A big part
of her wants to discover that the barn collapsing was
really an accident. I know better, though. An evil person is out there.*

And we're going to find him, or her.

*The ground around the location of the fire has been
trampled to the point that any potential evidence is
gone. I think I'll just stay up on the rail and walk around.
Try a different perspective.*

*Stephanie is checking the latches on the gates to see
if they open, and they do. And here comes the fire chief
to talk to her. Good, he can tell her if the fire was set
deliberately.*

*I'll saunter over and eavesdrop. Wait a minute!
There's a little piece of material here on the fence. It
looks like some kind of stretchy nylon, like the kind of
blouses the barrel racing women were wearing, the kind
of blouse that hugs their bodies tight. It's blue and black.*

*Now all I have to do is match this material to a
rider and I'll have a good lead on the arsonist. Some-*

times, it pays to be a cat. The fire chief is looking over this way, so I'll just sharpen my claws in the railing and detach the material. It's so easy to fool the bipeds.

STEPHANIE FELT TRUE RELIEF as Hank came toward her. "I had our team moved to tenth place," he said, holding out his hand to the fire chief. "How are you, Dave?"

"Fine," Chief Adams said. "Looks like Miss Chisholm has herself an arsonist, though."

Hank nodded. "Could be some kids, just got carried away back here."

Stephanie took her cue from Hank. He obviously didn't want to let on to Chief Adams that they were having difficulties. She understood that Hank was protecting the future of the rodeo. No one would want to come and participate in a rodeo where there was a chance of fire or some other hazard.

"Could you tell how the fire started?" Stephanie asked the fireman.

"The wood is so dry, it was easy to start. We couldn't find any evidence of gasoline or anything like that. Could be as simple as Hank says, someone walked by and threw a lit cigarette." He shrugged. "Then again, it could have been deliberate." He looked at Stephanie. "You're Albert and Emily's niece, aren't you?"

"Yes, sir," she said, feeling again the constriction of life in a small town.

"I hear you're trying to hang on to the ranch."

One thing about Chief Adams, he was blunt. "Yes,

sir, I intend to hang on to it, as my aunt and uncle asked me to." She made it clear she had a valid claim.

"I didn't make it to the funeral, but the whole town is buzzing with gossip."

She didn't say anything, but she felt Hank's hand take hers and squeeze it. "It's not anyone's business but my own," she said.

"It becomes my business where a fire is set—if this one was set." He watched her carefully as he waited. "We've been having a rash of unexplained fires here in Pecos. You wouldn't know anything about that, would you?"

"Stephanie has only been in town this week. It would seem you'd have more business talking with the person who set the fire—if it was set," Hank said with emphasis. "Stephanie is simply trying to revive the rodeo, something this town desperately needs." There was an edge to Hank's voice as he put his arm around Stephanie's shoulders.

Chief Adams looked around at the arena. "I wish you luck, Miss Chisholm. The town does need a rodeo. We need to keep the ranches going, instead of going under. But there's little I can do about that. Just be careful, and stay alert. If someone is setting fires, there's no telling what else they might do."

He shook her hand and then Hank's before he walked away. "What do you make of that?" Stephanie asked Hank.

"It's hard to tell," Hank admitted. "I thought at first he was trying to put the blame on you. Then at the end…" He watched the fireman get in the big red truck and pull off. Adams never turned around to look at them.

They heard the sound of hooves and looked up to see Jackie Benton riding hard toward them.

"Are you okay?" she called as she brought her horse to a skidding stop. "I just heard. I saw the cows running loose in the arena and I wondered what had happened, then someone said there was a fire and you were almost trampled. I was over on the other side behind the stands so I didn't see anything until the cows came running out in the arena and by then it was all over." She took several deep breaths. "So are you okay?"

"We're fine," Stephanie said, glad that Hank was standing there with his arm around her. "We're just fine. It was an accident." She watched Jackie closely. The woman seemed genuinely concerned.

"Good Lord, those cows could have killed both of you." Jackie glanced at Familiar, "And that black cat. What is he doing up here anyway?"

"Familiar is sort of the rodeo mascot, but don't worry, we're fine," Hank said. "And Familiar, too. He's doing just great."

"Where is that cat?" Jackie asked.

"He was here a moment ago." Stephanie looked for the feline. She wasn't surprised that he was completely gone. He had a way of slipping out of sight without drawing attention to himself.

"I'll have to go call Johnny on my cell phone and tell him about all the excitement," Jackie said.

"Don't bother."

She whirled around at the sound of the male voice

that came from behind her horse. Stephanie swung her gaze past the horse and inhaled sharply.

Johnny Benton stood not ten feet away. He was partially hidden by the horse's rump, but as she was staring at him he stepped out into the arena lights.

The entire left side of his face was been severely clawed.

"My goodness, Johnny," Stephanie said, pretending to be startled by the way his face had been savaged. "What happened to you?"

"Our little cat Gumbo clawed me a few days ago." He gave Jackie a black look. "I was trying to worm her and she just went berserk." He shook his head. "She came close to getting my eye. I guess I'm going to have to take the cat out and shoot it."

"No!" Stephanie blurted before anyone could say something else. She hated the way some people treated animals. "If you don't want the cat, I'll take it. In fact, I'll stop by tomorrow and pick up the cat."

Jackie's face showed interest. "You'd take the cat back to New York?"

Stephanie started to say something, but she felt the pressure of Hank's hand. "Well, yes. I'd take the cat wherever I ended up living."

Jackie's head tilted. "You sound like you're thinking of giving up the big city. From what Johnny told me, that fast-paced life was really important to you."

Stephanie saw the same question on Johnny's face, but concerns about the city weren't where her thoughts had settled. She looked around to see if Familiar was anywhere nearby. If the black cat would saunter up, he might recognize Johnny from the attempted burning of the barn. If he recognized him, Familiar would definitely show it.

"Are you giving up the city, Stephanie?" Johnny asked. His voice was soft, but his gaze focused on her and held her.

"I don't know, Johnny," she said.

"I never thought you'd leave," he said in that same soft voice. "I never thought you'd consider coming back to Pecos and living on a ranch."

"Things change. People change." She glanced at Hank. He was her future. Johnny Benton had been a part of her past. She looked back at Johnny. "I've changed. Have you, Johnny?"

She saw he was taken aback by her question. "I don't know, Stephanie. Sometimes I don't think I've changed, it's just that I've gotten older." He sighed and resettled his hat.

"I thought you were in Austin," Hank said to him.

"Austin?" He looked at his wife and frowned.

"We should get ready for our rides," Jackie said. "The seventh team is running now. Johnny can be our cheering squad."

"Perfect," Hank said as he took Stephanie's hand and led her toward the tethered horses.

Stephanie glanced once behind her to look for the cat, but there was no sign of Familiar at all, and Johnny Benton was staring at the ground as he followed his wife back to her horse trailer.

Chapter Seventeen

Hank stood in the doorway of the bedroom and looked at Stephanie as she slept. It was still dark outside, but soon it would be dawn, and he hoped she would sleep on. She was completely worn-out. And with just cause. She'd worked like a Trojan for the entire week and ridden like a champion at the rodeo. The team he'd ridden with her and Jackie had taken fastest time, penning the three cows in eighteen seconds flat. She'd been magnificent on Flicker, her substitute horse since Mirage was still under observation.

The rest of the night had gone off without a hitch, and by the time they'd made sure the cows were watered, hayed and put out on the little bit of pasture around the arena, it had been long after midnight.

Familiar had come up to them with a small scrap of blue and black material, but no one they'd seen had been wearing such a blouse. Hank had made sure to check all the riders as they came up to the gate, but he'd drawn a blank. The person who'd been wearing the blue blouse had either gone home before the team penning began or changed shirts, as Hank had done. Or else that person had never intended to ride in the rodeo, but had sneaked into the back of the arena, done the dirty deed and scattered. Hank could easily see the scenario go in either direction.

Stephanie turned over, and he went to the bed and sat down so that he could smooth the tangled curls from her face. She smiled in her sleep, and he was overcome with the desire to make love to her, but he held back. She looked exhausted, and the kindest thing he could do would be to allow her to rest. It was Saturday. The rodeo was over for another week. Rodney was in the barn and would feed and take care of the horses, and Hank had seen to Banjo. He had a sudden thought to go and get Biscuit. He'd been neglecting his own dog because he'd been so caught up in Stephanie's problems. Biscuit and Banjo were the best of friends, and no doubt Familiar would ignore Biscuit just as he did Banjo.

He picked up his pants, boots and keys, deciding that he'd run to his place for the heeler before Stephanie woke up. Maybe they'd take his dog and ride out to the creek. Take a picnic. Do a little skinny-dipping in the cold waters of the stream. He felt another rush of desire and had to force himself to leave the bedroom and the sleeping woman.

He'd just put his hand on the doorknob when he realized something was wrong. It was an inner warning, not specific at all. Then he heard the cat crying, and he realized the bedroom door was locked.

He twisted the knob hard, but he couldn't turn it. The ranch house was older, and the doors were solid oak. The hardware had been designed to last forever, and the locking mechanisms required old keys. Keys he'd never seen in any of the doors since he'd known the McCammons.

He thumped the door with his shoulder. He was more angry than worried—until he smelled smoke.

It was almost impossible, but he knew instantly that someone had set the house on fire. First the barn, then the arena, now the ranch house.

He put his shoulder to the door with force, but it was solid. The noise he'd made woke Stephanie and she sat up, panic on her face.

"What's wrong?" she asked.

"Get dressed," he said, fighting to stay calm.

"What is it?" She climbed out of bed and slid into her jeans. In another few seconds, she was dressed.

The scent of the fire was stronger, and Hank went to the bedroom window. A set of bars blocked the exit. He turned to her, calm but determined. "We have to get out. There's a fire."

"Fire!" The word was enough to panic her. "Here, in the house?" She picked up the bedside telephone, her face going even paler. "It's dead." She replaced the receiver. "Where is the fire?"

"I'm not certain. Somewhere near the bedroom door. I can smell it."

"Familiar! Banjo!" She rushed to the door and twisted the knob with all of her strength. "We have to save the animals."

"We have to save ourselves," Hank said. Then he remembered the trap door in the bedroom closet. He'd hammered a board across it, but that was nothing. He rushed to the closet and opened the doors. In a moment he had a shoehorn as a crowbar and a shoe as a hammer. It was tedious work, but he slowly began to loosen the nails in the board.

"I smell it stronger," Stephanie said. When she tried to touch the doorknob, she drew her hand back. "It's hot."

"They must have started the fire in the hallway," Hank said.

"Why didn't Banjo bark?" she asked.

He could see she dreaded the answer he might give. Banjo would have given a warning, unless the dog was injured or dead. "As soon as we get out of here, I'll try to find the dog. And the cat." He was worried about Familiar. The cat had extraordinary intelligence, and he was alert. How had the arsonist managed to catch the cat off guard?

Stephanie knelt beside him, and together they tugged on the loosened board until it came free. Hank pushed back the carpet and opened the trap door. He couldn't see anything but dark in the hole. "Go," he said.

Stephanie didn't hesitate. She dropped into the hole and onto her hands and knees. "It's so dark, I can't see which way to go."

Hank dropped down beside her. She was right. There was no indication which direction to take. "Follow me," he said as he led west, calculating that was the shortest way out from under the house.

As they began to crawl, he could feel the heat of the burning ranch house on his back. Stephanie didn't cry or complain, but he knew how much she was suffering. The ranch house was her home, the place she'd grown from a girl to a woman, and it was being destroyed above her. They had to get outside and then find a phone to call the fire department.

He believed the fire had been started outside her bedroom door. The clear intent was to kill her, and possibly him. Whoever was doing this wasn't content any longer with trying to frighten Stephanie away. The culprit wanted to kill her now. The stakes had risen dramatically.

He felt cool air on his face and he crawled forward. After four feet, he was outside, away from the house. Stephanie was right behind him and he helped her to her feet. The sound of sirens was distant, but at least someone, probably Rodney, had called. With such quick response, there was a chance the fire could be contained and stopped.

Cuddling Stephanie against his chest, he ran away from the house. When they were fifty yards distant, he turned back to look. Fire leapt from the windows in the central part of the house, but the roof was still intact.

"I'm going back for Familiar and Banjo," he said.

Stephanie grabbed his arm. "Hank, don't."

"I have to. I can't let them stay in there and die."

She nodded. "I'm coming, too."

"No." He grasped her shoulders. "No, Stephanie. Stay here. If it's too dangerous, I'll come back."

He turned and ran before she could protest. He was

about to kick in the back door when he heard Banjo
barking. He gave the door a mighty kick. Right beside
the dog was Familiar. Both looked slightly disoriented,
and Hank knew instantly how the arsonist and gotten
past them—they'd been drugged.

Putting one animal under each arm, he hefted them
and dashed back to Stephanie. She cradled the dog and
stroked his head while he checked Familiar over.

"What's wrong with them?" Stephanie asked.

"They've been drugged." The cat was fighting
against the sedation. "I think they'll be okay."

"Aunt Em would be devastated," she said. "The Mc-
Cammon family has lived here for such a long time.
Now the ranch house is burning."

"The fire truck should be here—"Before he could
finish he saw the lights swing down the driveway. The
truck was followed by several cars, folks who'd heard
the alarm and had come to help.

In a matter of seconds the yard was filled with men
shouting as the hoses were unreeled and water sprayed
on the house.

"What happened?" Chief Adams asked as he came
over to them.

"We're not certain," Hank said.

"It's time to stop playing around," Adams said, an
edge to his voice. "Someone is trying to injure one or
both of you. Now it's time you were straight with me
before this goes any further."

Hank saw Stephanie looking at him, asking him what
she should do. He nodded. The fire chief had seen the

evidence for himself. There was no point trying to skirt the truth now.

"Someone is trying to injure us," Stephanie said. "Someone who wants to run me off this ranch so that I'll drop my claim to it."

"I suggest you get a really good lawyer and take this up with the judge first thing Monday morning." Adams focused on the firemen fighting the blaze. "We'll save the farmhouse, but there's a lot of damage. Whoever is behind all of these fires needs to be stopped. Now."

"Thanks," Hank said. "We're going to follow your advice to the letter." It was time to resolve the issue before Stephanie was hurt worse than she had been. Hank didn't trust the law or the court system, but now he had no other recourse. And he knew just who to call to make sure Stephanie got the best representation possible.

STEPHANIE HELD BACK the tears, but she felt as if her broken heart had just been slashed to ribbons. Aunt Em's lovely old hardwood floor was ruined, as were the walls in the hallway and so many other things.

As Hank had pointed out, though, they were safe, the animals were safe and the will was safe. So now, on Sunday afternoon, she sat in the law offices of Lorry Dalton in Dallas, waiting while the lawyer read over the will.

She could see it was a struggle for Lorry not to keep looking at her son. There was a rift there, but Stephanie had no idea what it might be. Hank had said little about his mother. Stephanie knew she had left Jared Dalton and pursued a law career in Dallas. She could see in Hank that the loss of his mother had had a profound impact on the man he'd become. Some of the impact good, some not so good.

She watched the lawyer as she reached for a law book and began to do some research. Lorry had tawny hair, thick and perfectly cut. She had Hank's green eyes, and his smile. When Lorry finally looked up at Stephanie, her gaze slid to Hank and then back.

"You have pretty good grounds if we can determine how Peebles got your aunt and uncle to sign the will."

"How can we do that?" Stephanie asked. It seemed insurmountable, actually. How could she possibly get the lawyer to confess to a criminal act?

"If he frightened or fraudulently led your relatives, then he's done it to other people. Chances are many of them are dead, like the cases you found yourself. But I'd be willing to stake my life on the fact that some elderly couple still living has experienced the same thing. You just have to find them."

"Before the hearing in the morning," Hank said darkly.

"Before the hearing," Lorry said.

"That's the help you can give us?" Hank didn't try to hide his disappointment.

"I'm a lawyer, not a magician," Lorry said evenly. She looked at Stephanie. "My entire life I've been a bitter disappointment to my son. I'd hoped that was changing when he called me, but I see it hasn't." She stood up. "Miss Chisholm, I think you should hire legal counsel elsewhere."

"Ms. Dalton." Stephanie rose in one fluid motion. "I want you." She looked at Hank. "Hank said you were the best. I want you."

Lorry gave them both a calculated look. "I can't work miracles, I can only fight as hard as I can."

Stephanie nodded. "We'll find someone who used Peebles." She glanced at her watch. "We have almost fourteen hours. Will you be in Pecos tomorrow at ten?"

"Wild horses couldn't keep me away," Lorry said. She turned to her son. "Whatever happens, Hank, don't let this woman get away. If you have to follow her to Timbuktu, don't lose her. She's worth more than a million ranches."

Lorry pulled a map from the drawer of her desk. "This is an ownership map for all of the ranches around McCammon Ranch," she said as she handed it to Stephanie. "I'd start my search with lands adjoining McCammon."

"Why?" Hank asked.

"McCammon is the largest single ranch left in the area. I can't be certain, but I believe this is all a plan to develop the whole part of the county. McCammon land would be the key piece to get, but there are other, smaller pieces that are also vital." She tapped one section in particular. "Todd Murphy. See how his land is a narrow, thin strip. Try him first."

Stephanie grasped the older woman's hand. "Thank you, Ms. Dalton."

"Call me Lorry," she said. "If I'm really lucky, one day you might even call me Mom."

FAMILIAR YOWLED when he heard Hank's and Stephanie's voices. They'd left him and Banjo at Doc Smith's for safekeeping.

"I'll be glad that noisy feline is going home," Doc said. He grinned. "Both he and Banjo are fine, though I have to say that cat is one of the worst patients I've ever had."

"Could you tell what they'd been given?" Stephanie asked.

"Some type of barbiturate. I'd guess it was put in some food."

"Familiar wouldn't eat anything from a stranger," Stephanie said.

"Then you gave it to him, unbeknownst."

Stephanie thought back to the things she'd given Familiar to eat. She knew exactly then. "The concession at the rodeo! After everything was over, Familiar was starving. I gave him some barbecue ribs, and then I brought some of the meat home for Banjo."

Hank looked stunned, and when he spoke, she finally understood why.

"Maizy?" he asked. "You think Maizy put some type of barbiturate in food for the cat?"

"I don't know," Stephanie answered honestly. "It could have been her. Or, it could have been someone who heard me order for the cat." She touched his hand. "Everyone in town knows I get food for Familiar, and then I told Maizy that it was for the cat and Banjo. Someone could have overheard me."

"Did you see anyone else around?"

She thought about it. "No, but they could have been behind the concession booth. I wasn't paying a lot of attention. I was tired, and Familiar was hungry."

Doc stroked the black cat's sleek fur. "They weren't trying to kill him or Banjo, just dope 'em up real good."

"So they could burn to death in a fire," Stephanie said bitterly. "I'm just surprised they didn't drug us, too." Her face when ashen. "Wait a minute. I fell asleep so hard, if you hadn't frightened me awake, I would have slept through it all."

Hank's face was tight with anger. "You bought a barbecue sandwich for me," he said. "I threw it away. I was too tired and still queasy from the smoke to eat."

"Get it," Doc said. "Send it over here and I'll test it for drugs."

"You got it," Stephanie said as they gathered Familiar and Banjo and left.

The dog and cat didn't seem the worse for wear. Familiar had his paws on the dash and was intently listening to everything Stephanie told him. When she got out the map and showed him the Murphy place, he patted it with his paw.

"He wants to go there now," Stephanie said. In the week she'd known Familiar, she was getting good at reading his wishes.

"We should go home and see how the repair crew is doing."

"Me-ow!" It was a regal command.

"Familiar says to go to the Murphy's." Stephanie

couldn't help smiling as she conveyed Familiar's adamant command.

"I see. Well, just who's in charge of this investigation?" Hank asked.

"Familiar," Stephanie said at the same time the cat gave an indignant hiss.

"I guess he is," Hank said. He turned down Ellen Drive and headed for the address he'd read on the map. The road narrowed and began to twist and turn, but he kept driving.

"Do you see that?" Stephanie asked pointing out the front windshield.

"What?"

"That little curl of smoke," she said.

Hank gunned the vehicle forward, making Familiar fight to keep his balance. Stephanie realized then that he feared that the Murphy family had been beset by arsonists, just as she'd been.

She gripped the door handle as the pickup careened left, then right, and spun in the sand as it rounded a corner. Hank drove all out, pushing the vehicle to the maximum of its maneuverability.

When they turned down the last stretch of driveway, she clearly saw the smoke. It was coming from the small stone ranch house, a place that looked as old as the McCammon ranch house.

"Damn," Hank said as he parked the truck beneath a tree and opened the door.

"Hank!" Stephanie got out, too, but she stood at the open door of the vehicle. The fire was hot. Intensely hot.

She couldn't tell if anyone was alive in the house. There weren't any vehicles in sight, so perhaps the Murphys had gone into town to church or to visit friends.

Hank was almost to the door when she heard the sound of a gunshot. Dirt kicked up at Hank's feet, and she saw him dive forward and roll onto the porch. He took cover behind a large rocking chair.

Another shot came, slamming into the truck by her head. She yelped and jumped into the truck, covering Familiar and Banjo as she ducked low.

"There's a gun behind the truck seat," Hank called to her. "Get it!"

She wiggled out the door enough so she could reach behind the seat and find the rifle. She pulled it out, cocked it and knelt behind the truck fender, looking for the shooter.

"I'll get the gun," Hank said, and she saw him rise to his feet.

"No!" She raised the rifle. "Stay there, Hank. He'll kill you if you try to cross the open yard." Behind Hank the fire was growing fiercer. She could see the smoke had darkened. Any moment, the house would go up like kindling. If anyone was in there, it would be too late.

"Hank, try to save the people in the house!"

He hesitated for several seconds, then he kicked the front door in and disappeared in a cloud of smoke. Familiar was right on his heels. The black cat darted into the burning house and disappeared from sight.

Stephanie checked the gun to be sure it was loaded. It was a hunting rifle with a good scope, and she brought it to her eye. What had seemed a long distance away was clear in the scope. She searched the area she believed the shots had come from for several minutes before she saw someone move.

She didn't recognize the shooter, and she didn't want to. Her finger curled around the trigger of the gun. She sighted her target just as the man stood up to shoot down at her again. She took a breath and began to slowly exhale as she focused on his right shoulder and squeezed off the shot.

It seemed slow motion as the man dropped his rifle, grabbed his shoulder and spun backward.

She'd got him!

Chapter Eighteen

Stephanie looked Sheriff Sam Hodges straight in the eye and answered all of his questions. Jail didn't intimidate her—the knowledge that she'd shot a man, possibly killed him, was the worst punishment anyone could inflict on her. That Nate Peebles had been trying to kill her, and Hank, and Todd Murphy didn't diminish the horror of what she'd done. She sat in the hospital waiting room, preparing herself for word that the man she'd shot was dead.

Familiar, too, was missing. The last she'd seen of him was when he ran into Todd Murphy's burning house. After an ambulance had come and taken Peebles and Murphy to the hospital, she and Hank had searched high and low for the cat, but there was no sign of him anywhere until just before they were ready to leave. The cat had a smudged piece of paper in his mouth. Todd Murphy's copy of his will, and in it was a clause leaving the ranch to none other than Nate Peebles. To Stephanie, it was all the proof she needed.

The door to the waiting room opened and a doctor stepped inside. He glanced at the sheriff, Hank and her. "Peebles lost a lot of blood. He's unconscious, and he may not come out of it," he said.

"What about Murphy?" the sheriff asked.

"He's in a lot worse shape. Smoke inhalation almost got him. If Mr. Dalton hadn't gotten him out of the house, he would have died in the next few minutes. Who did the CPR?"

Hank nodded at Stephanie. "She did."

"You saved his life," the doctor said.

Sheriff Davis nodded. "Thanks, Dr. Simpson." He dismissed the doctor by turning back to face Stephanie. "Now tell me everything, and then we're going to go over it again and again and again until I'm satisfied that I know every detail."

When Stephanie was finished, the sheriff sat back in his chair. His eyes narrowed as he gazed first at Stephanie and then at Hank.

"You should have come to me," he said.

Hank shook his head. "We didn't know who to trust."

"Well you're going to trust me now. As the fire chief told you, there's been a lot of fires around here lately. Without evidence, I can't bring any charges, but I'll just say that it makes sense to me that Albert and Emily were killed the way they were because if they'd died in a fire, I would have put it all together."

"So you believe us?" Stephanie asked.

He nodded. "I do, and I have an idea how we're going to settle all of this. We need some physical evidence."

"We have the glove and the test results Doc Smith ran on the DNA," Hank said.

"And the will from Todd Murphy that Familiar found."

"Which won't do us any good to prove Peebles as a scoundrel unless Mr. Murphy comes around enough to tell me *how* Peebles tricked him. We still have nothing to tie it all to Johnny Benton."

Stephanie realized the sheriff had a valid point. Her face brightened. "I know someone who can get it."

"Who?" the sheriff asked.

Hank pointed at the big black cat waiting beside Stephanie. "You won't believe us, but we'll show you."

The sheriff considered. "I don't have anything to lose by trying," he agreed.

STEPHANIE STOOD on the porch of the Johnny Benton home holding platters and an empty cake container. Familiar waited at her feet as she rang the doorbell.

Jackie came to the door and opened it. "Why, Stephanie, what brings you here?" There was a hint of annoyance in her voice. "I'm a little busy."

"I came to return the dishes you brought over after the funeral," Stephanie said. She stepped forward so that she was blocking the door open.

Hank watched the tableaux from behind a grove of oaks with the sheriff. He grinned as Familiar slipped inside the house while Jackie was busy with the dishes.

"I hope you're right about that cat," the sheriff said. "It's the golderndest thing I ever heard of."

"Trust me, Sheriff," Hank said, remembering his disbelief when Stephanie had first told him about Familiar. "The cat is amazing. We just have to give him room to work."

"A cat! If it was a dog, I'd be more confident. But a cat! Everyone knows cats are independent and unreliable."

"You'll see," Hank said. "Now just watch."

He focused his attention back on the ranch house. Stephanie stood in the doorway despite Jackie's best efforts to get her to leave.

"I just wanted to thank you for supporting the rodeo," Stephanie told her.

"No problem." Jackie put her hand on the door and closed it a little.

"Where were you when the fire started?" Stephanie asked.

Hank tensed. Stephanie was getting to the meat of it now. He hoped Familiar was successful in his search of the house.

"I was warming up for the team penning."

"Really. Were you wearing a blue and black shirt?"

"No." Jackie tried to look thoughtful, but her gaze moved across the lawn, determining if Stephanie had come alone.

"Was Wanda Hempstead wearing a blue and black blouse at some time that night?"

"How would I know? Who's this Wanda person anyway?" Jackie was getting belligerent.

"Jackie, I did a little searching around and I was astounded to discover that Wanda is your sister."

"What are you implying?" Jackie asked, alert. Her body was tensed, ready for action.

"That maybe you or your sister started the fire at the arena, as well as the fire at my home and the Todd Murphy fire."

Jackie paled. "You think I did that?"

"You or your husband." Stephanie put it right on the line.

Jackie shook her head. "There's something wrong with Johnny. Has been for a long time."

"Something like what?" Stephanie asked.

"He's been mean, and so greedy." She put a fist to her mouth. "I've tried to stand by him, but it's just no good. He's always comparing what he has to other people, and then he gets angry."

"That must be very hard," Stephanie said.

Hank couldn't tell if Stephanie believed Jackie or was merely acting her part. His body was so tense he felt that with the slightest provocation, he would explode. No one was certain what role Jackie played in the whole situation, but he didn't trust her, or her husband.

Jackie took another look around the yard. "Why don't you come inside, Stephanie. I'll make us some iced tea."

"Sounds lovely," Stephanie said, stepping through the doorway.

Hank started forward, until he felt the sheriff's hand on his arm.

"Let her go," the sheriff said. "She's a smart gal. She knows what she's doing."

"We can't protect her in there," Hank argued.

The sheriff shook his head. "We don't need to protest her, son. She can take care of herself. We just have to trust her now."

The front door closed, shutting Stephanie in and Hank out.

"WHERE'S JOHNNY?" Stephanie asked as she stepped into the kitchen.

"Why, you—" Jackie swung her fist at Stephanie's face.

Stephanie feinted right, then ducked under Jackie's arm, grabbed it and twisted it behind the woman's back. She was inside the house, and she intended to take full advantage of it.

"Where's Johnny?" she asked, giving Jackie's arm a bit of an upward twist just to show she meant business.

"Me-ow!" Familiar's cry came from down the hallway.

Stephanie pushed Jackie in front of her as she began to search for the cat.

"Let me go." Jackie twisted, trying to wiggle free.

Stephanie levered her arm up and heard Jackie's gasp of pain. "I've had it with you. You've tried to burn my horses, my barn, my arena, my cat and dog and my home. Now I'm going to find out the truth and how you're involved in this, and I don't care how much I have to hurt you to get to it."

She pushed Jackie forward down the hallway.

"Meow!"

She could hear Familiar's excited cry, and she

paused outside the doorway of what had to be a bedroom. "Familiar?"

"Meow!"

He was inside. She pushed the door open and stalled in the hallway. Johnny Benton, his face dripping fresh blood, was tied to a chair. Familiar was on the bed beside him. Next to the cat was a blue and black barrel racer's Western shirt with a hole in the sleeve.

"Me-ow!" The cat darted past Johnny and headed behind the door.

Stephanie realized just in the nick of time what was happening. She pushed Jackie forward hard enough so that she stumbled into her husband and they both went crashing to the floor. Wanda Hempstead leapt out from behind the door, a hammer in her hand. She made a wild swing at Stephanie, but tripped on the tangle of her sister and brother-in-law.

As she fought to regain her balance, Familiar launched himself at her.

Wanda gave up the fight almost instantly. She dropped the hammer and began batting at her head where Familiar hung tight will all four paws.

"Get him off! Get him off!" She screamed and whirled around the room.

Stephanie watched in amazement. Wanda was terrified of the cat. Absolutely terrified.

Jackie made an attempt to get to her feet, but Stephanie forestalled it. She put her foot on Jackie's rump and pushed her back down to the floor. "I advise you to stay there," she said, "or Familiar will take care of you."

She heard running footsteps and Hank and the sheriff came barreling into the room. It didn't take the sheriff long to put the cuffs on Jackie, and Wanda put up no resistance once Familiar was removed from her scalp.

"If I ever get a chance, I'm going to kill that cat," she said bitterly as she was led out of the room by the deputies the sheriff had on standby.

Jackie was cuffed and taken out after her sister. Hank and Stephanie untied Johnny and helped him to his feet. He held out his hands for the cuffs.

The sheriff looked at him. "Let's go in the kitchen and make some coffee," he said. "I'm not sure I have all of this straight in my head."

They filed into the kitchen, and while Stephanie made the coffee, Johnny told his story. Jackie had wanted more and more, things he wasn't financially able to give her, but she'd pushed him until he had nothing else to give.

"I didn't have it figured out until the business with the gasoline," Johnny said. He looked at Stephanie and wasn't able to hold her gaze. "I never thought she'd really do anything to hurt anyone. She was greedy, but I never thought she'd bring harm to anyone."

"What about the fire?" Hank prompted. He sat at the table with the sheriff and Johnny.

"I heard her talking to someone on the phone last week. I realized after listening a few minutes she was going to try to start a fire. So I followed her that night. When she went up to the barn at McCammon Ranch, I followed her inside. I was up there fighting with her when Hank came into the barn. I had no idea she had a gun. When she fired at Hank, I pushed her down the ladder. Before I could follow her, the cat jumped me. Then I had to go back and try to retrieve the gas tanks. I didn't mean to hurt Rodney, but I had to get away."

Hank nodded. "It could have gone that way," he said.

"I only wanted to stop Jackie from doing something terrible. But then it got worse. I began to pay more attention, and I saw that she was in way over her head. Her and her sister." He said the last bitterly. "Wanda Nell is bad news, too. Those two thought of everything."

"How did Nate Peebles fit into all of this?" Stephanie asked.

"He was in love with Jackie. Oh, they tried to pretend it was Wanda Nell, but it was Jackie. Jackie said she was doing all of this to get the McCammon land. When I finally saw the will and realized it was going to Peebles, I knew she was going to leave me as soon as he got that land. That's all she ever wanted, what she viewed as my assets."

He lowered his head. "I'm sorry, Stephanie. I suspect Wanda and Jackie were somehow responsible for the deaths of Albert and Emily." His head dropped lower. "I never thought she could do something that bad."

Stephanie felt pity for Johnny. Pity and relief. She'd been so afraid that it was him, the man her uncle had befriended for so many years.

"Did you realize Jackie and Wanda were trying to frame you?" she asked gently. She recalled the night she'd seen Johnny—or someone dressed like him—go to Nate Peebles' home.

He shook his head. "No, but I'm not surprised. That's how they were going to get away with everything. Then she'd be free of me and have all the land." His eyes were bleak. "I was just a fool, I guess."

"Not such a fool," Hank said. "Wanda planted a glove with your blood on it in the barn, trying to implicate you in the collapse of it."

"They had it all figured out," he said.

"But not well enough to outsmart Familiar," Stephanie said, picking up the black cat and kissing him.

"Looks like you folks are set for the reading of the will in the morning," the sheriff said. "That's a civil matter and none of my concern, so I'll just take Mr. Benton on down to the jail."

"Are you charging him with something?" Stephanie asked as she released a struggling Familiar to the floor.

"I'm not sure yet," the sheriff said. "Depends on what else I find out. But one thing for certain, he'll be right where I need him, if I need him."

Stephanie watched the sheriff load Johnny into the truck, and then she felt Familiar's paw tugging at her jeans.

"He has something to show us," Hank said. He picked the cat up from the floor. "Let's go."

Stephanie and Hank are obsessed with each other. The danger is done and now they're getting all oogly-eyed, but there is one more thing I want settled.

What in the heck did Wanda bury in the yard?

I could just about drive as easily as it is to get them to go where I need them to go, but at last we're here.

Wanda Nell Hempstead's house. And there's the shovel in the front yard. If I jump on it a few times, I'll make them understand I want it picked up. There, Hank has it. And now they're showing a little more interest as we rush to the backyard.

There's the hole. Hank has caught on. He's digging away. And here comes the plastic bag with the second bloody glove on it, and the box. Now Hank is whacking the box with the shovel, and there is it. One single piece of paper. Signed by Johnny Benton, leaving all of his possessions to his loving wife. Jackie wasn't taking any chances. She got her own husband to sign over everything he owned to her—and Nate Peebles was the lawyer who drew up the will.

Dang, she was going to bump Johnny off if he didn't take the fall. Whew! Talk about a critter that eats its mate! I can see Stephanie and Hank are jubilant. Well, we might as well get back to the ranch house, assess the damage and start on the cleanup. Stephanie won't ever leave Texas again, that much I can see.

Chapter Nineteen

Stephanie sat at the long mahogany table and looked in the judge's sour face. She held three wills in her hand, but she still wasn't certain she would have justice. Not even with Nate Peebles charged with attempted murder.

Hank sat beside her, with Familiar on the other side. At the head of the table, beside the judge, was Lorry Dalton, Hank's mother, ready to do battle. A bevy of reporters, arranged by Ms. Dalton, waited outside the judge's chamber for her to exit. To Stephanie's left was Todd Murphy, in a wheelchair with an oxygen tank, but spitting fire.

She knew her aunt and uncle's document by heart, but the will that Familiar had saved from the Todd Murphy residence was icing on the cake. In the will Murphy had signed over his property to Nate Peebles—except that Todd Murphy was alive and fully able to dispute the will.

The judge called everything to order and in deference to Todd Murphy's delicate health, he asked him to speak first.

"That scoundrel Peebles wrote up the will the way I told him, and then he brought another copy for me to sign," Murphy said. "I didn't read it too closely, 'cause I figured it was what I told him, not that stuff he made up."

Lorry pulled a sheaf of papers from her briefcase. "As Mr. Murphy indicates, Mr. Peebles was in the habit of tricking his clients. I have eleven additional wills where this is very likely the case. I submit them to you, Judge, for further study."

"Thank you, counselor," the judge said. "Go on, Mr. Murphy."

"It's a dang good thing that cat found the will and got it out of the house, otherwise we wouldn't have the evidence we need," Murphy said angrily. "It wasn't enough that he tried to steal my land, he was going to burn me to death to boot! That cat saved me."

"Yes," Stephanie said, stroking the cat. "He's an amazing feline."

The judge ordered everyone to be silent while he read over the wills Lorry Dalton presented him. One was the copy of the will she claimed to be valid for McCammon Ranch. Another was Todd Murphy's will, and a third was the will Familiar had found buried in Wanda's backyard.

She saw the judge frown and look up. The door opened and the sheriff stepped into the room. "Judge, I've got someone who would like to talk to you."

"Right now?" the judge asked angrily.

"This will bear on the will," the sheriff promised. The door opened wider and Nate Peebles, his right shoulder bandaged, stepped into the room. "Nate, here, has cut a deal," the sheriff said. "As part of that deal, he's going to tell you all about that will he has inheriting McCammon Ranch."

All of the arrogance had disappeared from the lawyer. He took a chair and cleared his throat.

"I suggest you start talking," the judge said.

"I falsified the will," he said. "For Albert and Emily McCammon. I did that. Like I did for Mr. Murphy. It was a simple matter of putting the wrong document down for them to sign."

"Because they trusted you, an officer of the court," the judge said scathingly.

"That's right." He swallowed. "But I didn't have anything to do with killing the McCammons. That was Jackie. The McCammons were renovating the barn. It was easy enough for Jackie to saw through the timbers when no one was watching her. Then she and her sister lured the McCammons out there on the pretext of talking about decorating the apartments. She used a tractor to pull the barn down on them."

Peebles looked at the judge. "Your honor, I fell in love with Jackie Benton. She was going to divorce her husband and marry me, but she wouldn't do it unless I had the land."

Stephanie felt as if a million ants were biting the top of her head. She'd never fainted in her life, but she knew she was close. Hank put his arm around her and handed her a glass of water while the judge ordered everyone to shut up.

When Stephanie had calmed down, the judge pointed

at Peebles. "You're going to jail for a long time. A very long time. Your girlfriend probably won't see freedom again in her lifetime. Nor will her sister, Ms. Hempstead." He turned to Stephanie. "The will presented by Mr. Peebles is hereby ruled invalid. I accept the will you presented. And I'm going to go back and look at every will Mr. Peebles has written for the past five years." He stood up. "You are all dismissed."

Lorry Dalton leaned in to Stephanie. "You didn't need me at all, but I'm glad I was here to witness this. You've won, Stephanie. McCammon Ranch is yours."

HANK TOOK OFF HIS HAT and let the wind cool his head as he galloped beside Stephanie. They'd ridden the McCammon land from one end to the other, and Stephanie had plans and more plans. It was wonderful to listen to her dreams of the future. Dreams that included him.

He waved her over to the creek that had been part of why he'd gone to meet her in the first place. Twisty Creek. It had certainly been a twisty adventure they'd shared. With lots of disappointments and heartache for Stephanie. The good news was that the ranch house was already under repair and the contractor assured them it would be just like it was before.

Rio stepped closer to Mirage as they stood in the shade. "We're going to have some wonderful years ahead of us," he said.

"I know." She looked over the vista that was her family's land. "I can feel it."

"Together," he said.

She smiled. "Is that cowboy lingo for some kind of proposal?"

He laughed. "No. I'm going to propose to you. But I'm going to do it right and proper over a bottle of champagne and some kind of French food that we'll have to go to Dallas to get."

"Maybe we can find a place that delivers," Stephanie said.

"All the way here?" Hank lifted his eyebrows. "Maybe."

"Or maybe we could just get Maizy to pack up a picnic lunch. Without the tranquilizers someone slipped into her food."

"She was appalled," Hank said. "Must have been Wanda or Jackie when Maizy wasn't looking."

"I don't need French cooking or a fancy restaurant."

"I hope you're sure about that," Hank said. "That Friday night rodeo is going to be a demanding master."

"I know." She leaned over and kissed him. "Now let's go make sure Familiar catches his flight. He's got folks who love him waiting to pick him up at the airport."

"He's some kind of cat, isn't he?" Hank asked. "I wish he'd stay."

"Me, too, but he has other cases to solve."

I've grown to hate goodbyes. I love my humanoids, Peter and Eleanor, but I could stay here with Hank and Stephanie. I could become a cowcat—as long as no one made me ride a horse! But I could have a Jeep, something like that.